The
Christkindl's Gift

Kathleen Morgan

Revell
Grand Rapids, Michigan

© 2004 by Kathleen Morgan

Published by Fleming H. Revell
a division of Baker Publishing Group
P.O. Box 6287, Grand Rapids, MI 49516-6287
www.bakerbooks.com

Printed in the United States of America

Library of Congress Cataloging-in-Publication Data
Morgan, Kathleen, 1950-
    The Christkindl's gift / Kathleen Morgan.
        p.   cm.
    ISBN 0-8007-1871-2 (cloth)
    1. Widows—Fiction. 2. Cowboys—Fiction. 3. Single mothers—Fiction. I. Title.
PS3563.08647C486 2004
813'.54—dc22   2004004885

Scripture is taken from the King James Version of the Bible.

In memory of my grandmother,
Anna Hannack Ehlert

Your sins are forgiven you for His name's sake.
1 John 2:12

Colorado, December 5, 1913

"Erich. Erich! Wake up. *Es ist Sankt Nikolausabend!*"

At the insistent voice and small hand shaking him by the shoulder, he rolled over. His seven-year-old sister, Rosa, clutched one of her pale blond braids in her fist, while the other hung loose and all but undone. Clad in a long-sleeved white nightgown, she knelt beside him on his bed. Outside, the wan December sun was, even now, barely illuminating the new day.

He groaned. "Go back to sleep, Rosa. It's too early to get up."

"But, Erich! It's St. Nicholas Eve! Don't you care?"

Erich grabbed at his pillow, pulling it from beneath him to cover his head. Nicholas Eve was the night when St. Nicholas, carrying his crozier and dressed in his red cloak and gold bishop's mitre, came with gifts. "Of course I care," he growled from beneath his pillow. "I'll just care more when I'm fully awake."

"*Ach*, Erich. You're such a big *Dummkopf!*" With a tug, his sister wrenched the pillow from his head. "I have an idea. A most wonderful idea!"

It was hopeless, Erich thought. Further sleep was out of the question. "And what might that most wonderful idea be?" he asked with his best long-suffering, ten-year-old brother tone.

Rosa giggled. "You know you want to hear my idea. You know it, Erich Hannack!"

He flipped back over, eyed her with lifted brow, then pulled free the braid end that was now in his sister's mouth. The tip was wet and dark gold. "That's so disgusting. Why do you suck on your hair?"

She shrugged, unperturbed. "Because it makes me feel good and helps me think. Why else?"

"Well, tell me about your most wonderful idea, will you? Before you have to stick the whole braid in your mouth, anyway."

"I wouldn't do that. That's disgusting!"

Erich rolled his eyes. "The idea, Rosa. Tell me the idea."

"*Ja, ja.*" As if settling in for an extended sojourn, Rosa moved closer, sat on her heels, and folded her hands demurely in her lap. "Do you remember last night when *Grossvater* told us the story about *Sankt Nikolaus?*"

"Grandfather *always* tells us that story the night before St. Nicholas Eve. You know that, Rosa."

"*Ja,*"—her small head bobbed in agreement—"but this time he also told us that some children write letters to give to *Sankt Nikolaus*. Letters for the *Christkindl.*"

"And St. Nicholas finds the children's letters and takes them to the Christ Child, and leaves behind nuts, sweets, and gifts in the shoes of all good girls and boys." Erich yawned hugely. "So, what's all that to us?"

Rosa began to bounce on the bed, grinning. "We need to write the *Christkindl* a letter, of course. A letter asking Him to bring us a new *Vater*."

Erich jerked up, nearly knocking his sister off the bed. "A new father? Are you crazy in the head? *Mutti* would never—"

"She'd have to, if the Baby Jesus sent him. Wouldn't she, Erich?"

His sister had a point. Their mother was always saying how important it was to take whatever God gave you and be thankful for it. But this was a very big, and very important, gift.

He scratched his head. "Well, maybe she would. And it isn't as if *Mutti* isn't lonely. Sometimes, when she thinks I'm not looking, she still cries. I know she misses Father. And Grandfather could sure use help with all the ranch work. I try, but I'm just not big or strong enough yet. And he's not been feeling well these past few months."

"Well, I'm lonely too." Rosa slipped her braid end back into the corner of her mouth. "I miss having a *Vater*. Someone to sing me to sleep when *Mutti*'s too busy to do it. Someone to carry me on his shoulders. And now that it's winter, someone to pull me on my sled." She nodded resolutely. "*Ja*, we need a new *Vater*."

The more Erich considered it, the more he knew his sister was right. Who would've thought such an idea could come from a girl, and a very small girl at that? But it had, and he wasn't such a *Dummkopf* that he'd ignore a wonderful idea, no matter its source.

"*Ja,* you're right, Rosa." His mind racing, Erich drew up his legs and rested his chin on his knees. "We *do* need a new father. And who better than the *Christkindl* to send us the perfect one?"

"*Mutti, Mutti! Es schneit. Es schneit!*"

Hearing her daughter's excited cry later that afternoon, Anna Hannack glanced up from the loaf of bread she was kneading. Beyond the lace curtains framing the ranch house's kitchen windows, fat, white flakes were indeed floating lazily by. She smiled, wiped her flour-coated hands on her apron, and walked to where her daughter stood with her button nose pressed to the rapidly frosting glass.

"Yes, Rosa," Anna said, putting extra emphasis on the words, "*it is snowing.* You must remember to speak the English, not German."

"*Ach,* she knows the words well enough, *Mutti,*" Erich muttered from his seat at the other end of the kitchen table. "She just gets excited and forgets. She sucks on her hair and forgets to speak English all the time at school. And then the other children are very quick to correct her."

Anna frowned and glanced back at her son. Ever since the death of Anna's husband, Karl, a year and a half ago, her daughter had reverted to some of her more childish behaviors. "But not in an unkind way, I hope? The other students don't make Rosa feel bad or cry, do they?"

Erich shrugged. "Most don't, but then many of them at least know *Deutsch,* even if they don't speak it."

"German, Erich. It's called German in America."

"Ja, ja." Her son expelled an exasperated breath and returned to the wooden horse he was carving. "I know."

With a soft chuckle, Anna turned back to her daughter. "Look how fast the snow falls, Rosa. We'll soon be covered in a blanket of white."

"But, *Mutti.*" Rosa wheeled about so quickly her braids all but slapped her cheeks. "How will *Sankt Nikolaus* travel through the snow? What if he gets l-lost and cannot find our h-house tonight?" Her rosebud mouth trembled, and tears filled her bright blue eyes.

Tonight was *Nicholasabend.* Rosa and Erich already had their best pair of shoes cleaned and polished. The children were awaiting but their bedtime this evening to place the shoes on the covered front porch. The Advent wreath notwithstanding, as far as the children were concerned, St. Nicholas Eve truly marked the beginning of the Christmas season.

Anna laid a hand on her daughter's shoulder. "Don't worry, *Liebling,*" she crooned, using the German word for darling. "St. Nicholas will find our house. If need be, the *Christkindl* will show him the way."

"The Christ Child had certainly better." Erich glanced up from his intent work and cast a dark look at the snow, which was now coming down even harder and faster. "We have an important message for St. Nicholas to take to Him. And it *has* to be delivered before Christmas Eve, it does."

"*Ja,*" Rosa piped up, nodding her head in fervent agreement. "It has to, *Mutti.* It just *has* to!"

Their mother eyed them, her mouth quirking in bemusement. Though the custom of writing notes to the Child Jesus wasn't uncommon, neither of her two children had ever done so in the past. Not in Germany, where they had lived until three and a half years ago when their father had gotten it into his head to immigrate to America in the hopes of attaining a better life for them all. And not in the Christmases since then on their small ranch outside the thriving German town of Wolffsburg, Colorado.

But then, Anna recalled with a sharp pang, Karl had always been the incurable dreamer and eternal optimist in the family. Sweet, trusting Karl, gone now from their lives.

The old longing and pain welled up, threatening to squeeze what little joy she had managed finally to regain, threatening to squeeze it back into that all-too-familiar, aching lump in the middle of her chest. *Ach,* how she yearned to return to her beloved *Deutschland,* to the house in Rüdesheim with its wondrous views of the Rhine River and verdant, vineyard-covered hills! True, they had been poor, grindingly so, and there'd be no beloved Karl anymore to share it with, but at least there she'd be safe. There she'd belong.

Her father-in-law, however, wouldn't hear of it. There was nothing left for them in Germany, Anton Hannack had firmly informed her. Nothing but scant hope of a future for her or for his grandchildren. Would she shame her husband's name, belittle everything his son had ever wanted for his family, by turning her back on all they had already gained in coming to America? Give it a chance, Anton had urged. Trust in Karl's vision even if you cannot find one of your own. America's a wonderful land; we'll make our place here, you'll see.

But her father-in-law didn't understand. He hadn't lost his spouse in a strange, hostile land. Anton's wife died a peaceful death ten years ago, and not as a result of tragedy. In Christian charity Karl had taken in two men for a night, only to have the ungrateful wretches try to rob them in their sleep. Bleeding to death in his wife's arms, he struggled to the end to fathom why the men he welcomed had killed him.

She didn't care what her father-in-law said. She'd never trust a stranger again and, as far as she was concerned, America was and would always be a land of strangers.

"*Mutti?*" A sudden, sharp tug on her sleeve jerked Anna back to the present. She looked down into the stricken face of her daughter.

"*Ja,* Rosa? What is it now?"

"The letter for the *Christkindl.* We *must* get it to *Sankt Nikolaus.*"

Banishing her somber thoughts for her child's sake if not for her own, Anna laughed and knelt to meet Rosa's anxious gaze eye-to-eye. "And what could possibly be so important that, if need be, it couldn't wait for another year? Hmmm, *Liebling?*"

Rosa's eyes grew wide. "Well, we were going to ask—"

"Rosa! *Nein!*" Erich scraped back his chair, jumped up, and hurried over. "It's a wonderful surprise, *Mutti.* A wonderful surprise for us all. You'll have to wait until Christmas, though."

"I will, will I?" Anna glanced from one child to the other. Rosa's face was flushed; Erich's was pale. They were both hiding something. They were also very excited.

"Well, I suppose I can wait until Christmas," she said at last, not wishing to ruin whatever surprise was apparently so dear to the both of them. "*If* you can keep a secret as big as this one seems for that long."

Erich gave a whoop of laughter. "You'll just have to wait and see, won't you, *Mutti?*"

Anna grinned at her tousled-haired son, thinking, for one fleeting moment more, how much he looked like Karl with his snapping, dark brown eyes and light brown hair. *Ach, Karl, Karl,* she thought. *If only you were here, you'd be so proud of your son.*

Then she stood and headed back to the counter where her bread still waited. "*Ja,* I'll have to wait and see. In the meanwhile, though, I better get the bread in the oven, or supper won't be ready by the time your grandfather returns from town."

Her braid once more free of her mouth, Rosa hopped around on one foot until she reached her mother's side. "Maybe *Grossvater* will meet *Sankt Nikolaus* on the way and bring him home to us."

Erich snorted in disdain. "*Ach,* and sure that'll happen! What a big *Dummkopf* you are sometimes, Rosa."

2

It was well past dusk before Anton Hannack arrived home. Anna had just lit an oil lamp and placed it in the front window to help guide him when she saw the dark form of a wagon and team of horses appear from the whirling white that was now a blizzard. With a soft exclamation, she grabbed her jacket and a knit scarf for her head.

"*Grossvater* is home," she informed the two children, who were busy setting the kitchen table. "Erich, put on your hat and coat and come help us bring in the supplies. Rosa"—she halted her daughter in mid-step as the girl made a move for her own coat—"you finish setting the table. What with all the snow and mess, there'll be enough confusion with the three of us out there."

"*Ach, Mutti,*" the little girl wailed. "Why does Erich always have all the fun?"

"And since when is going out into the freezing wind and snow fun?" her brother grumbled, even as he shrugged into his coat and pulled his knit cap low over his ears and forehead.

"You both have your duties. Please see to them." Anna donned her own coat, wrapped the scarf about her head and neck, then, without a backward glance, headed to the front door.

Anton strode up as she opened it, his beard and mustache frosted with ice, his eyes dark with worry. "Hurry, Daughter." He turned, gestured to the back of the wagon. "I found a man . . . unconscious and half frozen . . . lying in the middle of Twisted Pine Road. We must get him inside and warmed before he dies."

Anna stopped dead in her tracks. *A man . . . another stranger . . . in her house?* Her breath caught in her throat. Suddenly, she couldn't breathe.

"N-nein," she whispered, shaking her head vehemently. "I cannot . . . I *will not* bring another stranger into my house." She gazed up at her father-in-law. "Please, Anton. I know how horrible this must sound, but please don't ask me to do this."

His glance hardened. "And would you turn away a brother in need, Daughter? Would you turn away an angel unaware?"

Sweet Jesus, Anna thought, lowering her head and clenching shut her eyes, *don't ask this of me. Not now. Not yet. I'm not ready.*

Yet, even as she lifted the desperate prayer heavenward, another voice seemed to intrude into her mind. *Trust Me,* it said. *Trust, and you will find all that you require.*

Trust . . . It was such a fragile thing, a frail thread spun between people, a gossamer strand cast to link one with life, one's hopes and dreams, and even with God. A thread irretrievably severed that horrible night she had lost Karl.

There was no trust left in her. Not even for God, a God who

had let such a good man as Karl die. A good man who, all the while, trusted and acted in His name.

"He's no brother to me," Anna ground out the words. "But he can stay the night if you promise he'll be gone in the morning. And only if you agree to tie him, hand and foot, to the bed."

Anton groaned. "The poor man's unconscious. He's no danger—"

"He'll not enter my house otherwise!" Hysteria edged her voice. "It's not just you and me we're endangering here, Anton. It's the children, and I won't risk losing them too. I'll do anything for you, but I won't do that. I won't!"

"*Ach,* Daughter, calm yourself." As the door opened behind them and Erich walked out, her father-in-law took her arm and gave it a warning squeeze. "It'll be as you ask. I promise."

Erich stepped up beside them. "Why are you two standing outside like this? What's wrong?"

Leave it to her ever-perceptive son immediately to notice the tension-laden atmosphere. Anna forced a weak smile. "*Grossvater* has found some poor man on the road. He's hurt, and we were just deciding what to do with him."

Immediately, her son's happy expression changed to one of wariness. "Do we know him? Is he someone from town?"

Anna shot Anton a sharp look before turning back to her son. "*Nein,* I don't think so. But we'll keep a very close eye on him tonight and take him to town tomorrow. Then the sheriff can decide what to do with him."

A bitter wind blew down just then, setting the snow again to whirling. Erich shivered. "Well, then I guess we need to bring him inside."

"*Ja,* that we should," his grandfather said. "Come now, you two. Help me carry this man into the house."

Anton and Erich immediately headed for the back of the wagon. After a moment more, Anna followed.

He was tall, hard-muscled but lean, and Anna guessed him to be about thirty. His face was pale and drawn; a large, purpling bruise marred the left side of his forehead. He wore boots and Levis, a long-sleeved knit undershirt, a plaid flannel shirt, gloves, and a lined leather jacket. His dark Stetson lay beside him in the wagon bed.

She looked around the back of the wagon. It was empty save for the boxes of supplies Anton had brought back from town. "That's all he had? Just the clothes on his back?"

"It appears so. If he rode a horse, it was nowhere to be found in this blizzard." The old man gestured to the unconscious cowboy. "Why don't you and Erich take his legs, and I'll carry his head and arms? It's past time we get him into the house."

Anna was surprised how difficult it was moving a tall man, especially one so limp. Finally, though, after several awkward moments when she feared they might drop him, the man was safely deposited in Erich's bedroom. As she helped Anton pull off the stranger's boots and jacket, she noticed a bullet hole in the jacket's left upper back. Anna turned to her son.

"Get a pillow and extra blankets from the cupboard and gather up whatever you'll need for the night. You can sleep with *Grossvater.*" She graced Anton with a narrow, challenging look. "Can't he, *Grossvater?*"

Her father-in-law's mouth quirked slightly. "Of course he can. It'll be a special treat for the both of us, it will."

Erich's face brightened. As if fearing his mother might yet change her mind, he hurriedly retrieved what he needed and left the room. Anna shut the bedroom door behind him.

When her son was out of earshot, she pulled the covers over the man, then stepped back. "Did you see the bullet wound in his back?"

Anton nodded. "*Ja,* but there was little blood, thanks to the cold, and not much I could do about it until I got him back here." He glanced toward the figure in Erich's bed. "Shall I go for the *Doktor?*"

Anna gave a firm shake of her head. "Not yet. I don't want you out in this weather if it isn't needed, and I might be able to remove the bullet myself. As discreetly as possible, so the children don't realize what you're doing, just gather up the supplies I'll need."

"I'll send Erich out to fetch the boxes and put up the horses. And I'm certain I can find something to distract Rosa too."

"One thing more," she said as her father-in-law turned toward the door. "I also need rope, an extra blanket, and Karl's pistol. Once all that's taken care of, supper is ready. You and the children can eat. Then have them wash up and head to bed."

"And what of you, Daughter? What do you intend to do?"

Her gaze strayed to the brown-haired man in her son's bed. Her mouth tightened. "I've no appetite, and now that *he's* in my house, I doubt I'd sleep anyway tonight. Once I get him patched up, I'll keep watch. In case he awakens, I mean," she hurried to explain when her father-in-law frowned. "In case he needs something. In case he's not quite the angel unaware you seem to think he might be."

Fortunately for both Anna and the stranger, his bullet wasn't difficult to remove. She soon had the spent slug out and the wound bandaged. Equally as fortunate, the entry site was clean, and the bullet appeared to have missed any vital organs. If infection didn't set in, the stranger had a very good chance of recovery.

In the end, though, the man's fate was in God's hands. At that admission, guilt stabbed through Anna. She should offer up a prayer for his healing, she well knew. As much as his unexpected arrival had stirred anew the memories of that horrible night she lost Karl, Anna's more pragmatic side warned that her tragedy hadn't been this poor man's fault. He might well be innocent of any wrongdoing even in being shot. He might even be a decent, honorable person.

And isn't that why you finally agreed to take him in? she asked herself between clenched teeth as she turned the man more squarely on his good side. She bunched a pillow behind his hips and shoulders to keep him off his back. *Because, in good conscience, you couldn't turn away someone in need?*

Still, her unsettled heart and chaotic emotions found little consolation in that admission. All she really wanted, Anna thought as she walked back around the bed to take a seat in the rocking chair, was for this man to have a miraculous recovery and leave tomorrow. Now *that* would be a gift truly worthy of St. Nicholas. It was still *Sankt Nikolausabend,* she recalled. She must remind Anton where she had hidden the treats to be put into the children's shoes after they went to bed. *Ach,* if only St. Nicholas brought gifts for the parents as well as for the children . . .

A cursory glance at the stranger confirmed he remained unconscious. Or more accurately, Anna amended, he was sleeping peacefully, if the utter calm of his expression and the gentle droop of his lower lip were any indication. He had a full, generous mouth, she realized with a sudden start of surprise. Indeed, he was actually quite attractive, with his strong, straight nose and high cheekbones accentuated by dark brows and lashes and wavy, chestnut hair.

She found herself wondering what color his eyes were and how they would look when they finally opened. Would they be kind, intelligent, and bright with life? Or would his good looks belie a slower intellect and less exalted ambitions? Or perhaps, she forced herself to consider the direst possibilities, he'd even be brutal and vulgar, not to mention greedy and dishonest.

Her glance strayed to the handgun and pieces of rope lying on the dresser across from the foot of the bed. Best she tie him now, before he awakened. Anna rose and retrieved the pieces of rope. Still, when she returned to the bed and knelt beside him, she caught herself hesitating.

It seemed so cruel to bind his hands. Yet what choice had she? Her family's welfare was potentially at stake. And she could not—*would not*—make the same error her husband had made. She was always the practical one, the family realist. It was she who had always tried to peer beneath the surface of people's actions to search for their true motivations.

Because of that Karl had affectionately called her his little cynic, but Anna had never taken offense. Why should she, when in her heart she knew she was right? Time and again, though she wished it were otherwise, she had seen how easily others were led solely by self-interest.

That realization only reinforced her intent to protect her family at all costs from this newest threat. Anna quickly made a slipknot, then loosened its loop and shoved it over the man's right hand. After tying the other end to the bed frame, she made a second slipknot with another piece of rope. Sliding that knotted loop over his left hand, she carefully lifted his arm until it was above his head and tied the rope's free end to the nearest bedpost.

Stepping back, Anna examined her work. It wasn't the most pleasing sight, viewing an unconscious, helpless man tied like that, but she had taken great care to make sure the loops weren't too tight, and his left arm was essentially supported by his head. Besides, she'd check everything periodically throughout the night to preclude the loops becoming too tight. As long as the stranger didn't begin fighting his restraints, he should remain comfortable.

She headed to the bedroom door and opened it a crack. From the looks of the dishes stacked by the sink, supper had been served and finished. She scanned the living room. Anton and the children were curled up in the big wing chair before the fire, indulging in a bedtime story.

Anna watched Erich and Rosa for a moment, savoring the fleeting sense that, for them, all was as it had always been. A warm, lingering time spent together basking in the comforting affection of a grandfather's love, their eyes shining with excited anticipation of the morn to come, of shoes overflowing with candy, nuts, and a few small gifts. It was how it should be for children. No fear, no worry, no pain.

She had tried so hard all these years to protect her children, to shield them from life's harsh realities for as long as she could. It was what a good parent did—let children have a childhood. In the end, though, both she and Karl had failed. That failure ate at Anna, and most likely would for a long time to come.

She was all Rosa and Erich had now, besides Anton. But Anton, for all he tried to do, was cut from the same cloth as his son. When it came to the ways of the world, he was equally as naïve. But then, she thought as she quietly closed the door, Anton and Karl had been blessed. They were kind, loving people, as was Karl's mother.

They had never known what her life had been before she finally ran away and met Karl. They had never known, because she had always kept it a secret. A secret she intended, to her dying day, to hold close and never, ever, share.

3

Ian Sutherland regained consciousness in stages, each step more pleasant than the last. First, he sensed he was wrapped in some sort of a warm, snug cocoon. That warmth was soon replaced by a feeling of softness, of a mattress beneath him, a pillow under his head, and a light-as-a-feather comforter resting over him. And then, as his eyes slowly opened to hazy morning light, his gaze fell on a golden-haired angel sitting in a chair beside him.

She was asleep; that much he could tell from the sweep of long, dark lashes resting on a rosy cheek, her relaxed expression, and the gentle rise and fall of her chest. Momentary confusion flooded him. He had never heard of angels sleeping, but now he knew it must be true. She *had* to be an angel. There was no other explanation for the vision of feminine loveliness dozing so close by he could almost reach out and touch her.

An impulse to do just that filled him, but he was fearful if he did, this divine apparition would surely disappear. Unless, Ian was swift to correct himself, he *was* already in heaven. But to be in heaven—he swallowed hard—he'd have to be dead.

The consideration didn't please him. To be on the way home, back to Culdee Creek Ranch and his sister and adopted American family, and to have his life cut short so suddenly and violently hadn't been in his plans. Not that the good Lord above didn't have the right to call him Home whenever He wished. It was just that Ian had so much living left to do, so many dreams yet to fulfill.

Dreams like a place to call his own, work that meant something, and mayhap someday even a lass to take to wife. His glance slid appreciatively down the form of the beautiful woman sleeping so serenely in the rocking chair. *Aye,* Ian thought, *a lass exactly like her.*

Her skin was creamy and flawless, her nose slim with delicately flared nostrils. Her lips were stained a soft shade of rose and were elegantly shaped. Hers was a mouth meant for long and ardent kisses, he mused, his thoughts taking wing before he roughly jerked them back. Such considerations weren't meant for angels, after all.

Still, hers was a body that would tempt a saint. He lifted his gaze to the top of her blond head, her thick, shining hair braided into a single plait that curled down from the back of her neck to nestle along the length of her shoulder. She was slim but nicely rounded in all the womanly places, dressed in a white long-sleeved blouse and a dark green wool skirt. Black low-button boots completed her simple outfit.

The angel—if she truly was the age she appeared to be— looked in her late twenties. Ian liked that. He had long ago tired of tittering girls who had little of interest to offer, much less the necessary life experience required to say much of anything. He'd wager this exquisite creature would never have such a problem. *If* she wasn't an angel, of course.

But did angels wear wedding rings? The question flashed through his mind almost as soon as his gaze moved to her hands. It certainly looked like a wedding ring—a plain gold band on the fourth finger of her left hand. Indeed, he wondered as he attempted to prop himself up on his elbow, were angels supposed to wear any kind—

Almost as quickly as he tried to move his arms, he was jerked quickly back. Ian glanced down at his right hand. It was tied to the bed frame. He arched back to look at his left. It was tied to one of the headboard posts.

The sudden movement also set off a sharp pain in his left midback, sharp enough momentarily to take his breath away. "By mountain and sea!" he loudly groaned out the words.

The angel sat bolt upright. Her lids snapped open to reveal pale gray-blue eyes, strikingly framed by dark brown lashes. *"Lieber Himmel!"*

The unexpectedly foreign word gave Ian pause. *"Lieber Himmel?* What language is that? Indeed, where *am* I?"

Her eyes wide, her face gone white, she stared down at him for a long moment. "It's German," the woman finally replied, as serious as she could be, "and you're in Colorado, of course. You startled me, and all I said was 'good gracious me.' Or at least that's the translation into English."

"So, I'm not in heaven and ye're not an angel." His mouth quirked wryly. "Too bad. I was beginning to warm up to the idea, especially with ye as my angel."

She rolled her eyes. "You're speaking like a crazy man." She

24

leaned toward him and touched his forehead with the back of her hand. "You don't seem to have a fever, though."

"That's good news." Ian looked pointedly down at his right hand, then up at his left. "So now that ye're reassured I'm not half out of my head with fever, might ye not consider untying me?"

The woman flushed. "That's not why I tied you."

He arched a brow. "Then why ever for?"

Suddenly, she couldn't quite seem to meet his gaze. "My father-in-law found you unconscious in the snow and brought you here. I don't know you, and for all I know, you could be some killer. So it's quite simple really. I tied you for our safety."

"And ye've dangerous men frequently passing through these parts, do ye?" Ian sighed. "Well, let me assure ye I'm not dangerous. My name's Ian Sutherland. I'm on my way to Culdee Creek Ranch, which is a big cattle spread east of Colorado Springs. My sister's wed to the son of Culdee Creek's owner. Mayhap ye've heard of them—the MacKays?"

"*Nein.*" The woman shook her head. "But then we're rather isolated up here in this mountain valley." Her gaze narrowed. "And you don't sound at all American, by the way. What are you really? English? Irish?"

"Scots, lass," he muttered. "I'm Scots and from the Highland village of Culdee, to be exact. Though I've managed to reside in the United States almost as long as in Scotland."

"So you're now an American, are you?"

Ian shrugged. "Nay, leastwise not officially. But it's a fine country and all, and someday I might well become a citizen all nice and legal-like." He paused. "How about ye? How long have ye lived in America now, and are *ye* a citizen?"

She scowled. "That's really none of your concern, is it?"

"Well, if ye don't wish to tell me, I suppose it isn't." He forgot his hands were tied, tried to sit up again, and was rewarded by his bonds tightening even more. "Would it be too much to at least ask yer name, lass? So as how I'd be knowing who the kind woman was who took me in? And yer father-in-law's name as well, in case I ever get the chance to thank him for saving my life?"

She stood, and Ian, for a fleeting instant, thought she might turn and leave without answering. There wasn't a glimmer of warmth in her eyes. Indeed, they looked as frigid as the snow-capped mountain peaks rimming the high valley in which she apparently lived.

With a slow release of breath, however, the woman finally replied. "My name is Anna Hannack. My father-in-law is Anton Hannack. I've two children, Rosa and Erich."

"And yer husband?" He glanced at her left hand. "In case I might be meeting him sometime too?"

Anna stared down at him with a hard, glacial expression. "He's not here right now, but his name's Karl. And before you begin plotting any fiendish plans, just know he should be home anytime now. Best you head on out before he returns. He doesn't like strangers any more than I do."

"Well, that should make for a verra warm introduction." Unperturbed, Ian met her gaze. "So, should I assume that also means ye've no intention of untying me?"

His hostess gave a derisive snort. "In case you haven't realized it yet, this isn't some hotel, and you're not a guest."

With that, she turned on her heel and exited the bedroom.

Ian stared at the closed door. He had heard of the German propensity for blunt speech. Until this moment, though, he had never experienced it.

Now he knew exactly what everyone meant.

Her heart pounding in her chest, Anna leaned against the bedroom door. Why had she lied to Ian Sutherland? She *never* lied. But somehow, when he asked about Karl, she felt compelled to make it appear as if her husband were still alive.

She knew she had uttered the untruths on the spur of the moment with the intent of protecting her family. If this Scotsman—who sounded at the very least like an aimless drifter—ever suspected her family's only protection was an old man, there was no limit to the thoughts that might enter his head. As much as she hated to lie, she hoped God would understand. After all, with Karl gone, everything now rested on her shoulders. And she *must* protect her family at all costs.

Still, even the consideration that her actions might offend God made hot tears sting Anna's eyes. Once she had been such a good, devout girl. When had that changed?

It wasn't Karl's fault, neither by being married to him nor because of his death. Yet, as she had matured into womanhood as a wife and mother, it seemed her priorities had gradually shifted. Not that God hadn't remained important in her life. It was just that she didn't have the time she had once had to spend with Him in quiet prayer and reflection. She had obligations to her husband and children, and sometimes—in Germany at least—it was all they could do to keep food on the table.

Not that it had been any easier with the move to Colorado. Homesteading up here in the Wet Mountain Valley had been equally backbreaking. This time, though, they had been working their own land, building their home and the beginnings of their cattle ranch, and ensuring a future for their children.

It hadn't been Germany, but with Karl at her side it had been bearable.

Despite her best efforts to contain them, the tears welled and trickled down Anna's cheeks. She leaned her head back against the door and, for a brief instant, allowed the pent-up grief to overwhelm her. It was one thing she had learned in the past eighteen months—not to fight the pain, but to give in to it. Surrendering seemed to lessen the intensity and length of the grief, if only until the next time.

"Daughter, whatever is the matter?" A gruff but kindly voice intruded suddenly into Anna's sorrow. "Is he dead, then? Has the stranger died?"

Her eyes snapped open, and she hastily wiped away her tears. *"Nein."* Anna stepped away from the door. "He's actually better. He's awake."

Compassion filled Anton's eyes. *"Ach,* then it's that other pain. The heart pain."

The heart pain. That was the code phrase between them for when it became too much to bear—losing Karl—and they would tear up suddenly or just need a few private minutes to themselves.

"*Ja.* It's the heart pain."

He gestured to the bedroom door. "Does he need anything? I could stay with him until you're able to do so again."

"All he needs, or so he says, is to be untied," she replied with a grimace. "But I don't trust him, Anton. He's a drifter, a Scotsman who has lived in America almost as long as Scotland, though he claims to be a relative of some rancher near Colorado Springs. I don't think he's up to any good."

"And does this drifter have a name?"

"Ian Sutherland. But for all I know, he could've made that up."

Anton scratched his beard. "Well, we can't keep him tied forever. Might as well turn him over to the sheriff if we're going to do that."

"*Ja,* maybe we should." Anna brightened at the idea. "You could ride to Wolffsburg today and bring Sheriff Mahoney back with you. He could decide what to do with this man."

Her father-in-law laughed. "Have you looked outside yet this morning? Even in your eagerness to be rid of this Ian, I'm hoping you won't feel compelled to send me back out into that storm."

Anna's heart sank. She hurried to the living room window, parted the curtains, and glanced out. Evidently the snow that had begun yesterday afternoon had never abated, if the three- to four-foot layer on the front porch was any indication. Beyond that she couldn't differentiate anything, what with the dense, swirling mass of white that lay before her. It wasn't a fit day to send anyone out, be it man or beast.

She groaned. "*Ach,* it isn't fair. It just isn't fair!"

"Let me talk to this Ian Sutherland." Anton laid a hand on

her arm. "I've always been a fair judge of people. If I've any doubts about him, he'll stay tied up until he's able to leave or the sheriff comes for him."

Though Anna wasn't certain she totally agreed with Anton's assessment that he was a fair judge of people, at least he had never made a blunder the size Karl made that fateful night. Her father-in-law had gone to town for supplies that same day, and a torrential downpour had temporarily washed out the road leading home. Anton had been forced to spend the night in town.

Thinking back on it, Anna supposed she *should* be grateful her father-in-law hadn't been here. He might also have died in the ensuing gunfight. Then she and the children would've been left alone in a foreign land without any man to help them. Anton would've been of little assistance to Karl at any rate. He abhorred guns and knew next to nothing about how to use them.

That admission reminded Anna she had left Karl's loaded pistol on the dresser. If Ian Sutherland happened to see it and somehow managed to free himself . . .

"Fine," she ground out the word. "Come with me and I'll introduce you. Then, as far as I'm concerned, you two can talk the rest of the day away."

"That might be a pleasant distraction from the weather," the old man said, "but could you cook us some breakfast in the meanwhile? Fried potatoes and onions would do nicely, along with that delicious bread from last night. And maybe even a few bits of sausage?"

She supposed if this Ian must stay here at least another day, she'd have to feed him. Besides, some good food in his belly would help him heal all the more quickly, not to mention restore his strength. Not that she wanted him getting *too* strong before they turned him over to the sheriff.

"Ja, ja." Anna nodded curtly. "I'll make us all a big breakfast, though perhaps something a little lighter, like porridge, would sit better on this Ian's stomach for his first meal. One way or another, he stays in Erich's bedroom. I don't want him near the children."

Anton nodded. "A wise plan, at least for the time being. Until I can ascertain what sort of man this Ian Sutherland really is, at any rate."

A wise plan for the time being, Anna silently added with grim resolve, *and* up until he leaves, too. Erich and Rosa had been through more than any children needed to endure. Ian Sutherland would have nothing—absolutely nothing—to do with her children.

4

Anna wasted no time retrieving the pistol from the top of the dresser. She wasn't quick enough, though, in hiding it within her apron pocket. Ian saw it. He shot her a quizzical look when she finally lifted her gaze back to him.

"If ye kept that gun in here for protection against me, lass," he said, noting even as he spoke a stoutly built, grey-bearded man enter the room, "ye needn't have. I mean neither ye nor yer family any harm."

She blushed furiously. "You may say what you will, but in the end I'll be the judge of what I will or won't think of you. I don't know anything about—"

"Anna," the older man cut in gently just then, "weren't you going to see to our breakfast? I hear the children stirring, and I'm sure they'll be as hungry as the rest of us."

As if to protest, the beautiful German woman opened her mouth, then hesitated before snapping it shut just as swiftly. "*Ja,* best I check on the children," she muttered before all but flying across the room and exiting.

The older man then turned to Ian. "How do you feel?" He walked toward him, hand outstretched until his gaze fell on Ian's bound hands. His hand fell back to his side. "I'm called Anton, and Anna tells me you're Ian Sutherland."

Ian smiled thinly. "Aye, that I am. And I'm verra pleased to make yer acquaintance at long last. Yer daughter-in-law tells me ye're the one who found me and brought me here. I owe ye a great debt, I do. Indeed, if I wasn't quite so encumbered"—his mouth quirked wryly as he shot a quick look at his hands—"I'd begin by shaking yer hand. Unfortunately, Mrs. Hannack seems to have serious doubts about my motives, not to mention my integrity."

"Can you blame her for being cautious?" Anton asked as he pulled the rocking chair closer to the bed and sat. "You're not from these parts, and I found you unconscious and shot in the back. For all we know, you could be a bank robber or some outlaw."

"Aye, I suppose I could be. I almost wonder why ye even bothered to take me in."

Anton chuckled. "Well, for one thing, you would've surely frozen to death out there, what with being unconscious and lying exposed to the storm. And, for another, the good Lord admonishes us to take in strangers and care for the sick and needy. How could I possibly turn from you?"

So these people were Christians, Ian thought, or at least this Anton seemed to be. He wasn't so sure about Anna. Still, the realization comforted him. God was good and, despite Ian's occasional missteps, continued as steadfast and loving as ever.

"I thank ye for that, Anton," Ian said. "And thank the Lord

Jesus, as well, for men like ye. For what it's worth to ye, I also give *ye* my word I mean ye and yers no harm. On the contrary. I'll be forever in yer debt."

"You owe us nothing, Ian Sutherland. I'd have done the same for any man."

For a fleeting instant, Ian's thoughts turned once more to the beauteous Anna. If the choice had been solely hers, would *she* have been as willing to help him? Somehow, he sensed Anton had been the one who had insisted on taking him in. Though he couldn't fathom why, Anna was afraid of him. Deathly afraid.

"Has something happened to turn yer daughter-in-law against strangers?" He met the older man's gaze once more. "Or has she just taken some instant dislike to me in particular?"

"Anna has her reasons. It's not my place to speak of them, though, but hers."

"I see." Ian shifted on the bed. "Well, as soon as I'm able, I mean to be moving on. I don't wish to impose on yer hospitality any longer than need be. I've family of my own awaiting my arrival." He smiled. "I'm planning on spending Christmas with them, ye know."

"*Ach,* are you now?" Anton sniffed the air appreciatively, air that Ian suddenly noticed was laden with the tantalizing scent of frying sausage. "Then it's past time you were getting some good, hearty food into your belly." He rose and pushed back the rocker. "Give me a few moments, will you? I need to speak with my daughter-in-law."

"Do ye have any coffee?" Ian's stomach seemingly decided at that moment to growl. He gazed up at his host. "If ye do and it's no trouble, I could surely use a nice cup of strong, black coffee."

"Could you now? Well, *that* shouldn't be any problem at all. On the other hand, *drinking* the coffee might be. *Ja,* it could at that."

The old man grinned broadly. Ian was struck by how much Anton looked like some of the drawings he had seen of Santa Claus, what with his silver beard and thick silver brows, his kindly dark eyes, pink cheeks, and rotund belly. Ian frowned in puzzlement.

"And why would drinking a cup of coffee . . . ?" His voice faded as he recalled his bound hands. "Aye, I suppose ye're right. Mayhap I should forego the coffee after all."

"*Ja,* perhaps you should. But take heart. All might not yet be lost," Anton tossed over his shoulder as he headed for the bedroom door. "After all, everything's possible with the Lord. *Ja,* it most certainly is."

From the pile of snow tracked in on the rug by the front door to the excited whispers coming from the vicinity of the living-room fireplace, Anna could tell the children had already been outside to see what St. Nicholas had brought. She lifted a quick little prayer of thanksgiving that Anton had remembered to fill Erich and Rosa's shoes. The unexpected—and very much unwanted—arrival of Ian Sutherland last evening had thrown everything into turmoil. So much turmoil, leastwise for Anna, that Ian's continued presence threatened not only her peace of mind, but also the meticulous attention she tried always to pay to meeting her family's needs.

But that sort of upheaval wouldn't continue much longer. *Nein,* Anna resolved, squaring her shoulders and lifting her chin as she headed for the top kitchen cupboard where she always stored Karl's now unloaded gun. She meant to be rid of this roguish Scotsman just as soon as the weather cleared.

"Mutti! Mutti!" Rosa's voice rose in happy entreaty as Anna slid the pistol onto the highest cabinet shelf and closed the door. "Come see what *Sankt Nikolaus*—St. Nicholas, I mean—brought us. Come see!"

"In a minute, Rosa." Anna added a few pieces of fresh wood to the coals in the cast-iron cook stove, then laid two long, plump sausages into a frying pan and slid it onto the stove. "Let *Mutti* get the breakfast started first. Then I'll be right over."

She proceeded to retrieve six already baked potatoes from the icebox and slice them thinly. A generous glob of butter was then added to another fry pan, after which she tossed in the sliced potatoes, some chopped onion, and salt and pepper. That pan was placed as well on the rapidly heating stovetop. Finally, Anna filled a tea kettle with water from the sink hand pump and set it near the other vessels already on the stove.

The main preparations for breakfast begun, Anna wiped her hands on her apron and joined her children. Already Rosa had eaten at least three pieces of *chocolat,* if the brown smears around her mouth and three empty wrappers were any indication. Erich had also finished a piece of *chocolat* and was now industriously cracking nuts on the hearth with a small hammer. Besides the colorfully painted wooden top and a bag of marbles near Erich's right knee, Rosa held up a mesh bag filled with a ball and jacks in one hand and a box of colored chalks in the other.

"See, *Mutti?* Look what I got." An eager smile wreathed her daughter's face. "Will you play jacks with me, *Mutti?* Erich won't. He said it's a girl's game."

Anna sighed and shook her head. "Erich, that's not very kind."

"I'm sorry, Rosa." Her son hung his head. "I promise to play jacks with you at home, if you promise not to ask me to play them at school."

Rosa looked to her mother.

"That seems a fair trade, *Liebling*. Besides, at school you'll have plenty of other children who will most likely want to play with you."

"*Ja,*"—her daughter's expression brightened—"I will. There's Helga Thimm and Laura Metcalf and—"

The smell of frying sausage wafted to Anna's nose. "*Ja,* there'll be plenty of children." She turned and glanced toward the kitchen. "We'll talk more later. I have to get back to cooking breakfast now, before the sausages and potatoes burn."

"Don't let the sausages burn, *Mutti*." Erich glanced up from winding the string around his top. "You know how much I love your fried sausages."

"And fried potatoes, and bread with strawberry jam, and my scrambled eggs with cheese and onions and herbs," Anna added with a grin as she headed to the kitchen. "*Ja,* I know how much you love to eat most everything I cook, *Liebling.*"

A smile on her face, Anna finished making breakfast. Though she still had reservations about America, especially since Karl's death, she had to admit she loved her wonderful new log home. It had everything she could ever need—a spacious kitchen with its big cast-iron stove, sink pump, many cabinets, and a sink window view of gently undulating grassy meadows interspersed with stands of aspens and pines, a cozy living room with its rock-studded fireplace, four bedrooms, and an attic that not only provided a large play area for the children, but also served as a place to hang clothes in inclement weather. True, they had no electricity and had to use an outhouse, but Karl *had* been making inquiries of the town plumber as to the feasibility of indoor plumbing for a bathroom. Electricity, on the other hand, had yet to make it up to their high valley.

However she looked at it, their house was the height of luxury. Combined with the two hundred acres of grasslands that grew lush and rich in this mountain valley and the small herd of Herefords they had managed to purchase on credit, by German standards at the very least, they were rapidly becoming quite well-to-do. It wasn't enough, though, and hadn't been since she lost Karl.

Life had always been hard. Before she fell in love with Karl, Anna hadn't expected or allowed herself to dream of anything more than that. Life was but a vale of tears where one struggled and suffered, striving all the while to cling to one's faith in God and grow ever closer to Him. To hope for more than brief, fleeting moments of happiness was unrealistic, selfish even. Work—lots of hard work—and eventual death was all one could ever count on.

Karl had changed that for her. He was so kind, so good, and so full of the joy of life and living. He had never been selfish or begrudged anyone anything. He had just seen the world through different eyes. He loved God, loved his fellow man, and loved living.

According to Karl, life with all its unexpected beauty was God's gift, as was the happiness found in loving something or someone with your whole heart and soul. Life was bright, glorious, and rife with ennobling opportunities. Life was permeated with God, His presence found in every beat of one's heart, in every breath one breathed, in all that one experienced. And knowing that, Karl asked, believing that with all that one possessed, how could one *not* hold life close, clasping it to oneself like a lover does a beloved?

For over ten years, Anna had listened to her husband and had striven to see life as he had. Strangely enough, it hadn't been hard, leastwise not with a man such as Karl guiding her. Indeed, she had never known such happiness. She feared she never would again.

But then, how could she? It had all been a lie, an illusion. Life had never been beautiful. Life had been but waiting for Karl's brilliance to dim and fade. And, eventually, it had. No one could be so happy for long. Even God, it seemed, wouldn't permit that.

There had to be a reason—God *had to have a reason*—Anna thought as she perfunctorily dished the fried sausages then potatoes into bowls and prepared the eggs for scrambling. Even His Son had suffered and died on this earth. How could a sinner such as she expect any better?

If only she hadn't ever opened her heart to love, she might have been able to bear the life she had been given. But she *had* opened her heart. First with Karl, and then with the children she had so ardently and eagerly given him.

Love, however, was also mean and ugly. It stripped away all your defenses, laid bare your heart. And, in daring to love, you risked such terrible loss.

Just as Anna had feared, the void left in love's absence was even harder to bear than having never loved in the first place.

5

"Anna, we need to talk." Anton's deep voice intruded on her troubled thoughts a few minutes later. "It's inhumane to keep Ian tied like some animal."

"'Ian', is it now? Well, as far as I'm concerned, he may well *be* an animal." She refused to meet her father-in-law's gaze and, instead, focused on the eggs she was now scrambling. "Far better to keep him tied and my children protected. I'm sorry if he doesn't like it, but perhaps it'll hasten his recovery and subsequent departure."

"So, in the guise of guarding the children's safety from a man who means no one any harm, you risk frightening Erich and Rosa by keeping a guest in this house tied up? What message are you sending the children in doing this? That a man as dangerous as the men who killed their father is again in their midst? Well, not all men are like those who killed Karl, you know."

Aren't they? Anna thought. *Almost all the ones I've ever known, save you and Karl, were.*

Memories flooded her. Anger flared, and Anna's first impulse was to return the stinging recrimination with an equally severe retort of her own. But then good sense prevailed. Anton didn't know her past secrets, and after all he was, she reminded herself yet again, as blindly trusting as his son.

"The children don't need to see him. They're forbidden to—"

"Don't be an *Idiot*, Anna," her father-in-law hissed, glancing pointedly in the children's direction. "Sooner or later you've got to allow Ian out of his room and let Erich and Rosa meet him, or they'll start fabricating all sorts of horrible possibilities. You *know* they will, what with what happened . . ."

She clenched shut her eyes, her sense of helpless fury roiling within her. Anton was right about Erich and Rosa. Though she had tried her best to reweave the comforting, secure tapestry of home and family that had once enveloped them, her children were yet fragile. Fear and uncertainty remained like fraying, unwelcome threads, at the edge of all they said and did.

"Fine," she ground out between gritted teeth, "have it your way. But even when this man is feeling well enough to come out of his room, I still want him tied at night. I won't get a wink of sleep otherwise."

"Fair enough. But you'll have to be the one to tie him. I can't bring myself to do that."

If he thought to manipulate her by placing the onerous task on her shoulders, he was sadly mistaken. Anna finally looked up, impaling him with a steely gaze. "Well, *I* can and will."

Anton shrugged, a tiny smile tugging at the corner of his mouth. "I'll go free Ian then." He paused, glancing over Anna's shoulder to the frying pan. "Isn't it time to finish those eggs before they turn to rubber?"

Anna gasped and glanced down. The eggs were most definitely ready. "*Ja, ja.* Just go and tell your new friend the good news. Breakfast will be on the table when you return."

"And what of Ian's breakfast?"

"I'll make him some porridge after we finish eating. I still think that would be best for his stomach, what with this being his first meal after his injuries. And I'll make a good potato soup with leeks and bacon for lunch. He can try that with a slice of bread or two if he keeps down the porridge."

"One step at a time, *ja,* Daughter?"

She rolled her eyes. "*Ja,* one step after another until we have him heading out the door and on his way."

For all her hostility toward him, when it came to cooking, Ian had to give Anna Hannack her due. Though the day had started off rather poorly, with some bland, rather thin mixture she claimed was porridge, the potato soup at lunch had been rather tasty. And the supper he had finished just two hours ago had been downright delicious. The pot roast—which Anton informed him was called *Sauerbraten*—had been so tangy and succulently fork tender that, even now, Ian's mouth watered just thinking about it. The mashed potatoes and gravy, as well as the smoky-sweet red cabbage and apples, set off the meat to perfection. Not that he had found any fault in the bread pudding with hazelnuts for dessert either. Light and fluffy, it was the perfect end to a perfect meal.

Now he lay in bed atop a feather tick mattress, covered by a warm down comforter. Listening to the wind bluster and blow outside, Ian could almost imagine himself safe and snug at home. True, his back wound still smarted something fierce and his head continued to throb, but he was always one to count his blessings. He was alive; he would most likely survive his injuries, and he was basking in comfort rather than making a cold camp somewhere in this mountain wilderness.

God was good. He had, after all, guided a man like Anton to him in his time of need. And, for all her reluctance, Anna was an excellent nurse as well as cook. She had seen to dressing his wound this afternoon with great skill and gentleness, pronouncing him free of any signs of infection.

Ian had to admit he liked her touch, the feel of her long, finely wrought fingers on his skin. He also very much liked the pleasing scent of her hair as she had bent close to examine his wound. And her skin . . . Close up, Anna's complexion was as pure as rich cream, with the most subtle wash of rosy color on her cheeks.

Not that he dared stare at her for too long when she finally finished wrapping the bandage around his middle and proceeded to tie it off. No, he didn't dare risk stirring her suspicions or fears anew. Anton had barely managed, after all, to get her to agree to leave him untied during the day.

At the memory of the apologetic expression on the old man's face, Ian smiled. He imagined it had been a major victory getting Anna to agree even to that minor concession. He had already seen the flash of challenge in the blond Valkyrie's eyes a time or two. Challenge and a rock-hard resolve. Anna Hannack wasn't a woman any sane man dared purposely tangle with.

That said, it didn't mean he was adverse to a spirited woman. On the contrary. Ian liked his women full of vinegar and spice. It made life a lot more interesting. Those were also the sort of women who'd stand side by side with a man when the going got rough. Those were the sort who could be counted on to see things through, be it hardships and difficulties or a lifelong commitment.

Not that he was *looking* just yet for a lifelong commitment, Ian hastened to reassure himself. Especially not from some lass who might resemble this strange German woman, no matter how beautiful she was. He had been thinking about her positive attributes in theoretical terms, that's all. True, he had lifted desperate prayers to God when he had lain there in the snow after being shot. As he watched three men sneak down, steal his horse, and leave him to die, he prayed he'd survive and recover well enough to live a normal life. But if the truth be told, he most likely wasn't even the marrying kind.

"But Ye understand that, don't Ye, Lord?" he whispered, shoving to his elbows as he lifted his gaze heavenward. "Ye knew such thoughts were but the ravings of a desperate man? A man hardly suited to accomplish half of what Ye might ask of him?"

After a time, when no reply appeared to be forthcoming, Ian sighed and lowered himself back to the bed. To his chagrin, however, the unanswered questions remained. Though God might not hold him to his poorly considered ravings, the fact that *he* had made promises to amend his life and settle down once and for all disturbed him.

Disturbed him more than he cared to admit.

She hadn't realized how hard it would be, Anna thought as she drew up that evening outside Ian's bedroom. How hard it would be to continue to enter his room, talk to him, deal with him. And how hard it was going to be to tie him back to the bed this night.

In spite of her heated denial this morning, it *did* make her feel as if she were treating him like some animal. She could almost imagine, even now, his dark eyes searing clear through her as she did it. She could almost feel the scorching heat of his skin where she must touch him, slip the loops of rope around his wrists, and pull them tight.

Anna shuddered in revulsion. Yes, it *would* be hard, but nonetheless she was determined to see the onerous task through. She swallowed hard, lifted her chin, and knocked on the door.

"Come in," came a deep, masculine voice.

Before she could allow her cowardly misgivings to conquer her, Anna grabbed the doorknob, turned it, and walked in. Bathed in lamplight, Ian sat there in the rocker, his head turned slightly toward her.

"Is it time for the warden to lock up the prisoner for the night?" he asked dryly.

She flinched, then anger flared. "Whether you believe it or not, this isn't any more pleasant for me than it is for you. But it has to be done. I won't have a stranger loose in my house at night. Not ever again, anyway."

"But ye did once and lived to regret it? Is that what ye mean, lass?" Ian turned back to stare straight ahead and began gently to rock. "That someone ye trusted betrayed ye, and ye'll never let that happen again?"

Her anger escalated to fury. How dare he ask? How dare he make it sound like . . . like such a trivial thing? She had lost the love of her life, and all this man could do was demean her need to protect herself and her family?

"I don't owe you an explanation," she all but snarled. "Indeed, I don't owe you anything, you ungrateful, arrogant, disagreeable—"

"*Wheesht*, lass!" With a grimace of pain, Ian pushed from the rocker and took a few halting steps to stand before her. "I beg yer pardon. I didn't mean to make light of yer pain, whatever its source. And ye're right. Ye don't owe me aught. It's I who owe ye everything."

He was very tall, standing well over six feet in his stocking feet. Until now, Anna had only seen him sitting or lying flat in bed, and that was deceiving. He towered over her, making her feel small and helpless, even for her own five feet eight inches of height.

Perhaps it was his breadth of chest and shoulder, the powerful play of muscles in his unclothed, bandaged torso. Or perhaps, just perhaps, it was Ian's ruggedly attractive features and beard-shadowed jaw, both of which leant him a rakish, almost dangerous appearance. An appearance that was, at the same time, exciting stirring feelings, yearnings Anna had thought forever buried with her husband.

Nearly simultaneously with that shocking admission, shame flooded her. Hot blood scalded her cheeks. She couldn't bear to look at him and averted her gaze.

"Then, please," Anna whispered hoarsely. "Please, let's get this over. Don't make it any harder than it has to be—for either of us."

"So, it's hard on ye, too, lass?"

His breath wafted over her, setting her skin to tingling. She felt jittery, unsettled. The realization angered her anew.

"Despite your flippant words to the contrary, I'm not some inhumane warden." She lifted her gaze to his. "I've never done such a thing before in my life, and after you're gone, I pray to God I never have to again."

She gestured toward the bed. "Now, I weary of this pointless discussion. You agreed to cooperate, and I'm asking you to do so now. Will you, or won't you?"

He stared down at her for a long moment, his eyes so turbulent with myriad emotions she almost imagined drowning in their measureless depths. Then Ian nodded.

"As ye wish, lass." With that, he turned, took a few more faltering steps to the bed, and gingerly lowered himself onto it. He rolled on his right side, facing her. "If I must remain in one position this night, I prefer to sleep on my side."

Anna didn't want to know how he slept. Indeed, she didn't care to envision him sleeping at all. To allow herself to imagine Ian Sutherland, shirtless and clad only in his snug, well-worn Levis, was almost more than she could bear. It was all she could do even to grab the ropes from the top of the dresser and return to his side, where she proceeded hurriedly to bind his hands to the bed.

"Are the ropes comfortable enough?" she forced out past a

throat gone suddenly dry and constricted. "I don't want them too tight, after all."

Ian's mouth quirked slightly. "They're fine. I'll be okay, lass."

Now he apparently felt the need to comfort *her*, despite being the one treated so despicably. Tears rose to sting her eyes. "I'll check in on you before I head to bed—just to make sure you're still comfortable—and then first thing in the morning." She began to back toward the door. "G-good night."

The expression in his eyes sharpened to glittering awareness. "Good night, lass."

All but choking on a sob, she wheeled about and fled the room.

6

It had been decidedly uncomfortable sleeping in one position all night. Still, when Anna returned the next morning to release him, Ian said nothing as she untied his bonds. He stretched his cramped arms, then levered himself up in bed.

"Do you wish more porridge for breakfast?" she asked, making great efforts to avoid his gaze. "I hear tales you Scotsmen have a special affection for porridge."

"Aye, that we do." Ian chuckled. "Scots' porridge, however, is somewhat more substantial than what ye might consider porridge. For one thing, we use uncooked oatmeal, to which we add some boiling water and salt, then a generous dollop of milk or cream."

Anna gave a disdainful sniff. "Sounds more like food for pigs and cows than for people. I much prefer cooked farina with butter, sugar, milk, and cinnamon, or with fruit compote."

Ian shrugged. "Well, I suppose we all have our tastes. Mine just doesn't lean toward farina."

"So, what would you like?" Her hands lifted to fist on her hips. "I'm not running a hotel, you know."

"Aye, so ye've said." Ian grinned. "How about whatever ye and yer family are having, as long as it isn't porridge? And some of yer wonderful coffee?"

"We're having bread, sweet butter, cheese, and jams. It's commonly our breakfast, along with coffee, and milk for the children."

Though it didn't seem any hearty Scots' porridge was in the offing, Ian thought he could manage with what must be a typical German breakfast. He nodded. "That'll suit me fine. Shall I wash up and come out to the table?"

Anna opened her mouth to reply, then hesitation darkened her expression. She shook her head. "Best you eat in here. Until you're stronger, leastwise."

He was tempted to inform her that he was likely strong enough to walk a short distance from his room to the kitchen, but some instinct warned him Anna's real reasons were far different from the one she had given. Either she didn't want him getting a good look at the rest of the house, or she didn't want him meeting the children. Either way, nothing was served pushing the issue.

Ian scratched his jaw and was rewarded with the prickly feel of two days' worth of beard stubble. He could only wonder what the rest of his face looked like after the fall he had taken from his horse. "Do ye think I could borrow a razor and mirror after breakfast? Seems I lost mine when I was robbed, and I imagine a shave is long overdue. So as not to frighten yer children, if ever I should meet them."

She expelled a long, slow breath. "I'll see if I can find an extra razor somewhere." She turned to go.

"Lass?" Suddenly Ian didn't want her to leave.

Anna halted, then slowly faced him. "*Ja?* What is it?"

"Speaking of yer children? How old are they?"

The blood drained from her face, and Ian almost wished he could call back his words. But surely, sooner or later, he'd have reason to meet her children. Even if he didn't, Anna needed to get over her fear of him and whatever horrible things she imagined he might do. Showing an interest in her children, however mildly, might be a step in the right direction.

"Wh-why should you care?"

"Because I hear them talking sometimes, and it's quite evident I've taken over yer son's room." He cocked his head. "I mean nothing sinister by it, though. I'm just interested."

"*Ja.*" She swallowed hard and nodded. "I suppose there's no harm . . ."

"Nay, lass." Ian adjusted his voice to a gentle, soothing tone. "There's most definitely no harm."

"Erich." Anna lifted her chin and met his gaze. "He's ten and the oldest. And then there's Rosa. She's seven and a half."

It was progress of a sort, Ian imagined. He smiled. "Thank ye for that. And yer husband. Has he finally returned home?"

If her face had gone pale before, it turned positively pallid this time. "M-my husband?" She gave a shrill little laugh. "*Ach, nein.* The blizzard must have slowed his return. Most likely he'll be home today or tomorrow, though."

Something wasn't quite right, and that something had to do

with her husband. Still, Ian knew he trod on dangerous ground, and judged it best to drop the subject.

"Just as long as he returns safely," he said. "That's all that matters in the end, isn't it?"

"*J-ja,*" she stammered, casting a wild look over her shoulder. "I-I need to prepare breakfast."

The kind thing would be to allow Anna her escape. She looked so tightly wound, Ian feared she might snap. Besides, whatever he had said that upset her so apparently wasn't going to disappear anytime soon. Whatever it was, it also wasn't something easily dismissed. The question, though, was how deeply did he wish to delve into her personal affairs? He planned, after all, to be moving on just as soon as he could.

"Aye, I suppose ye do need to get on with breakfast," Ian said, trying to soften his words with a smile. "Don't let me keep ye from it."

She had almost given herself away when Ian asked about Karl's imminent return. She knew the reason why, too. She had never been, and never would be, a good liar.

Still, as she finished up the breakfast dishes and put the food away, Anna berated herself for lying. But the longer she kept the secret that she no longer had a husband, the greater the odds Ian Sutherland would leave before he ever found out. She sighed. *Ach, Lord, forgive me. I know I've no right to ask You to keep me strong in such an endeavor, but surely . . . surely . . .*

There was no excuse for her behavior. No excuse for the lying or the inhospitable way she continued to treat the man. She just truly didn't know what else to do. If she were to avoid an incident like the one that had taken Karl's life, trust and honesty were out of the question.

Ian claimed he meant her family no harm. He had looked sincere enough when he said it. Indeed, his eyes had shone with real interest when he asked about the children. But it could all be an act. It had been before.

Anna finished in the kitchen, removed her apron, and hung it on the peg by the back door. Her preoccupation with the right and wrong of Ian Sutherland's presence in her house was fast becoming tiresome. After all, there were far more important things to address this morning.

"Erich," she said, walking into the living room where her son and daughter were playing before the hearth, "time we were getting outside to help *Grossvater* with the chores. You can shovel the front porch and a walkway to the barn. I'll clear a path to the spring house."

Her son expelled a long-suffering breath. *"Ja, Mutti."* He paused to put away the marbles he had arranged in a big circle on the oak plank floor. "I'll get my boots and jacket." He rose, bag of marbles in hand, and sauntered down the hall to the enclosed back porch where they kept their boots and winter outerwear.

She watched him go, filled with such an intense love for her son that it was almost painful. Erich had had to grow up faster than Anna would've liked and assume responsibilities far beyond those usually required of children his age. True, Anton was now the male authority figure in the house, but he wasn't as strong or as able anymore as he liked to think. Anna saw how stiff and sore her father-in-law was first thing in the morning, how tentatively he now approached some of the more physically demanding ranch work. It was as if . . . as if something vital and life-sustaining had drained from him, as well, when Karl died.

Even Erich noticed the change in his grandfather. Not only had the boy mentioned it to her once, but he had also begun trying to shoulder more and more of the difficult chores. Problem was, though he was a strapping, strong lad for his meager ten years of age, there were some things that still exceeded his youthful capabilities.

She should consider hiring a man to help them with the ranch, Anna thought as she joined Erich on the back porch to pull on her own boots, a thick sweater, knit scarf, and cap before shoving into her jacket. Someone strongly built, like Ian Sutherland. Someone who knew his way around a ranch and wasn't afraid of hard work.

But *not* Ian Sutherland, she hastened to add as she donned her mittens. There was just something about him that gave her pause, something besides her innate mistrust of a stranger. For one thing, from some of the comments he had made—and not made—he didn't appear to be a man who liked long-term commitments. It was almost as if he were running from something. The question was, was it from something outside himself, or from within?

No, though she needed a strong young man to help her and Anton with the ranch, it had to be one whom she could depend upon through thick and thin. And, Anna thought as she recalled the handsome Scotsman standing so tall and powerful before her last night, she would lay odds dependability and stability weren't Ian Sutherland's strong suit.

From his spot in the rocking chair, Ian heard the front door slam shut and two pairs of booted feet tromp around on the front porch. He couldn't make out what they were saying, but from the tone of their voices, he quickly surmised one was Erich and the other Anna.

Ian knew Anton had already gone out to start the day's chores, now that the snow had finally stopped and the sun had begun to peek fitfully through occasional breaks in the clouds. First thing this morning, Ian had looked out the window and was greeted by a wonderland of snow-laden, dark green ponderosa and piñon pines, a thick blanket of whiteness, and the gray-brown, winter-barren bases of the Sangre de Cristo mountain range in the distance to the west.

It was beautiful country, of that there was no doubt. The pristine snow glinting like diamonds in the sunlight. The towering, majestic mountains. The rich contrast of dark evergreens with all the whiteness and clear, clean blue skies when the sun was in its fullest glory. Summers, especially late summers, he knew were equally glorious. That was when the wildflowers were at their height, and what abundance and variety of color bedecked the rich green grass then. The mountains of Colorado reminded him a lot of the mountains of his Highland home of Culdee.

Mayhap that was why, though he had lived and worked on Culdee Creek Ranch all those years of his youth, he always felt drawn to the Rocky Mountains. They were his Colorado

Highlands, he supposed. Ian sensed that all his answers—to those apparent questions and to those yet unspoken or unrecognized—would someday be found here.

He knew he always felt closest to God in the mountains. To Ian's way of thinking, they were, after all, God's greatest handiwork. They spoke to him of majesty, omnipotence, and eternity. They stirred his soul whenever he looked up at them. And they were one of the few things that filled him with peace, however transient that emotion might be in his life.

Mayhap that lack of peace, that restless yearning, though he didn't know for what, was the price he must pay for what he had done so long ago. Yet even as the memory of that horrible night sixteen years ago swamped him with renewed pain and regret, Ian flung it violently aside. It was in the past, he told himself. What he had done didn't make him a cold-blooded killer.

The harsh sound of a shovel scraping along the front porch, beneath his bedroom window and then past it, jolted Ian from his melancholy reverie. He leaned back in the old chair and began to rock. The motion soon soothed him, as did the dampened noise of the shovel moving up and down the length of the front porch. His lids drooped, the tension in his shoulders eased, and he felt himself drifting slowly toward sleep.

A loud crash somewhere outside his bedroom door jolted him awake. He cocked his head, listening. It had almost sounded like breaking glass. The noise didn't return, though. Mayhap he was just imagining things.

"*M-Mutti! Mutti,* come quick. *Ach,* come quick!"

The shoveling on the porch continued without any indication that the shoveler had heard the childish cry. Ian half rose from his chair, and his wound protested mightily. He lowered himself back into the rocker. Mayhap the little girl—for it was surely a girl's voice—had only cried out in horror at breaking something. If so, best he not—

"Mutti!" Rosa's voice came again. "H-help! I've cut myself."

Ignoring the stab of pain, Ian pushed from the chair. He took three quick steps toward the door, then caught himself as dizziness washed over him. For a long moment Ian stood there grasping the door frame for support and dragging in several deep, steadying breaths.

Finally, his head cleared. He opened the door and walked through, taking care to use whatever furniture stood between him and the kitchen. Once he was there, the room began to spin yet again, and Ian had to take a seat in one of the kitchen chairs.

"What's wrong, lass?" he said, fighting against the nausea that threatened to overpower him.

Rosa held her right hand, palm up, toward him. "I-I broke the sugar bowl. When I tried to pick up the pieces, I got glass in my hand. It hurts and it's bleeding."

It was most certainly bleeding, the red fluid pouring down her hand and through her fingers to fall in big, crimson drops on the floor. For a fleeting instant, Ian feared he might be sick. Then he drew in yet another deep breath and extended his hand.

"Come here, lass,"—he motioned her to him—"and let me have a closer look at it."

Rosa hesitated. "I don't know you, and *Mutti* told me never to go to strangers."

Irritation flooded Ian. Though he couldn't blame Anna for teaching her children caution around strangers, at the present moment a stranger was all that was available. He managed a friendly smile.

"My name's Ian Sutherland, and I'm the man yer grandfather took in the night of the blizzard. And now, since ye know my name and I already know yers because yer mither told me last night, we aren't really strangers anymore, are we?"

"Are you the man the *Christkindl* sent us?" A hopeful expression on her face, Rosa took a tentative step forward. "Because if you are, then I know you're not a stranger. You're a most wondrous gift."

Ian scowled in puzzlement. He had been called many things before, some not so very complimentary, but he had never been called a wondrous gift. An impulse to ask Rosa what she meant struck him, but he quashed it. Rosa needed her hand seen to, and likely her claims were naught more than childish ramblings.

"We're *all* gifts to each other, special blessings sent by the good Lord above to help each other." As he spoke, Ian motioned her forward. "And, just as yer grandfather was a gift to me, arriving at just the right time to save my life, I suppose I'm a gift back to him."

A sudden, doubtful look sprang into Rosa's bright blue eyes. She drew to a dead stop, and Ian regretted his silly hedging. "Aye, lass," he said with a sigh, "and I'm also a gift to ye, yer brother, and yer mither."

Rosa's mouth curved into a radiant smile. "*Ach,* I knew it! I knew it! Just wait until I tell Erich I was right. He'll be so mad that *he* didn't figure it out first."

The little girl closed the last few steps between them. "Now, will you fix my hand?" She thrust it toward him.

Ever so gently, Ian supported her wounded palm in his. The shard wasn't all that big, but its tip appeared to penetrate Rosa's hand about a quarter inch or so. He glanced up. "Where does yer mither keep her clean rags? Once I pull the glass free, yer hand will surely bleed even more fiercely."

The girl's eyes widened, but she turned and pointed to a drawer to the left of the sink. "In there. *Mutti* keeps her rags in there."

Ian measured the distance from the drawer and back to the chair. It'd be easier to pull the chair over so he could sit when he felt the need to and use the sink pump to flush Rosa's hand after he removed the shard. "Come along, lass." Gingerly, Ian shoved up from the chair and began to drag it along. "Let's go to the sink, shall we?"

Rosa nodded and, a trail of blood following her, headed toward the sink. Five minutes later Ian had the glass out and had flushed Rosa's hand. After taking his seat once more, he began tearing the cleanest rag into strips.

"Ye were verra braw, lass," he said, folding a wad of rag into a small compress and applying it over her wound. "If it'd been me, I think I'd have been yelling and jumping all over the place."

"*Ja,* my *mutti* tells me I'm a brave girl." Her little brows furrowed. "But what does 'braw' mean?"

He chuckled as he began to wrap the long strips around her hand. "Och, it means brave, lass. That's all."

She appeared to consider that a moment. "Well," Rosa said at last, "I don't think that's English. And besides, you sound kind of funny."

"That's because I'm Scots, lass, and speak the finest English of all." Ian finished tying off the bandage and looked up. "But I won't take offense if ye have to ask me to explain a word from time to time. In fact, maybe ye can teach me some German in the bargain."

Her head bobbed in avid agreement. "That sounds fair, especially since now that the *Christkindl* has sent you here—"

The front door opened just then. In stomped Anna, followed by Erich and Anton. As she approached the kitchen, Anna was the first to see Ian and Rosa. Her glance lowered to what Ian knew must be the trail of blood following in their wake. Her mouth dropped open; her rosy cheeks lost all their color, and she impaled Ian with a furious glare.

"What are you doing out of your room?" she cried. "And what, in the Good Lord's name, have you done to my daughter?"

7

Anna stared in horrified disbelief, uncertain whether to turn her ire on Ian or on her daughter, who stood so trustingly close to him. She finally decided Ian was old enough to know better.

"I asked you a question," she said, glaring at him. "What are you doing out of your room, and what did you do to my daughter?"

Rosa glanced uneasily from Ian to her mother, then held up her bandaged hand. "He fixed my hand, *Mutti*. I-I needed some sugar for my bread"—she indicated the slice of buttered bread sitting on a plate on the kitchen counter—"and the sugar bowl was in the cupboard. So I climbed up to get it, but then it fell and broke. I got a piece of glass in my hand trying to clean it up."

Her lower lip began to tremble. "I'm-I'm sorry, *Mutti*. I didn't mean to br-break it."

Once again, Anna's gaze swung to Ian's, then back to her daughter. "You shouldn't have disturbed Mr. Sutherland. He's still very ill. You should've come and gotten me."

"She tried to call for ye, lass," Ian said, apparently deciding it was time to join in the conversation. "However, what with all the scraping and stomping around going on outside, no one heard her. And I think, as well, she was afraid to cause yet more of a problem dripping blood across the house. So I came out to see what was wrong. She sounded quite frantic, after all."

"Oh . . . well . . . in that case, I suppose it all worked out for the best." Anna didn't know what else to say. Truth was, she was beginning to feel a tad embarrassed. She was also acutely aware her initially suspicious tone of voice and scalding stare hadn't been lost on Ian Sutherland.

"Do ye wish, then, for me to return to my room?" A slight smile twisted one corner of the big Scotsman's mouth. "Since I'm no longer needed—or wanted?"

Irritation rushed through her, and Anna barely contained another quelling glance. "You can sit there in the kitchen the rest of the day if you want to," she muttered. "If you feel you're up to it, that is."

Ian chuckled. "Well, actually, I'm thinking it took about all I had to get this far. Considering it was my first extended trek from my bed, ye know." He looked to Erich, who had closed the front door and come to stand protectively beside his mother. "Mayhap, if yer son's willing, he could help me back to my room."

"*Ja.*" Anna gave a curt nod. "It'll be hard to clean up the mess with you sitting in the middle of it." She turned to Erich. "*Liebling,* put away your coat and boots, then help Mr. Sutherland."

Her son eyed Ian with ill-disguised distrust, then nodded. "*Ja, Mutti.*"

Once the pair were finally headed to the bedroom, Anna

promptly forgot all about her unwanted guest. After removing her own jacket and boots, she hurried over to her daughter. "Let me see your hand." As she spoke, she took Rosa's hand and began untying her bandage.

The little girl attempted to pull away. "Don't, *Mutti*. He fixed it up all nice and neat. Don't ruin it."

There was an edge to Rosa's voice. It gave Anna pause. She stopped to look into her daughter's eyes. Confusion—and even a tinge of disappointment—burned there. But disappointment at what? Her treatment of Ian Sutherland? Her accusatory, ungrateful manner?

Shame filled her. It was one thing to make her doubts and dislike of Ian clear to him. It was quite another to display them before her children. Especially when the man had evidently begun to insinuate himself into Rosa's favor.

Anna sighed in frustration. And wasn't that exactly the reason she had wanted to keep her children away from Ian in the first place? Why she wanted him gone just as soon as it was humanly decent to send him on his way?

Her children—especially Rosa—were still so fragile. It would be so like her to reach out to any man close to Karl's age for the comfort, the father's love, she had lost and still craved. But, please God, not to Ian Sutherland. He surely wasn't a man to be trusted or counted on. He'd surely only wound, if not rebreak, her daughter's heart.

"I just want to make sure Mr. Sutherland did everything that needed to be done, *Liebling*," she said, forcing herself to return to the matter at hand. "If your cut is clean, I won't ruin the bandage. I just don't know him well enough to be certain he's any good at taking care of injuries, that's all."

Her daughter gave a small, indignant sniff. "Well, *I* know he did a good job. *I* watched him."

"*Ja,* you did." Ever so gently, Anna began once more to unwrap the bandage. "And, just as soon as I see what he did, I'll know too, won't I?"

"He's ever so kind, *Mutti.*" Rosa cocked her head and eyed her mother intently. "The *Christkindl* sent him, you know."

Anna's head jerked up. "The *Christkindl?* Whatever are you talking about, Rosa?"

"She's just being silly, *Mutti.*" Erich hurried down the hallway to the kitchen. "She gets these ideas . . . makes up silly stories sometimes. Don't you, Rosa?"

The little girl's eyes went huge as saucers. She nodded vehemently. "*Ja.* I make up stories." She sent her mother an anxious look. "It's all right, isn't it, *Mutti,* to make up stories?"

Anna glanced from Erich to Rosa. "*Ja,* making up stories for oneself is fine. Making up stories for the purpose of deceiving another, however, is lying."

"Well, claiming the *Christkindl* sent Mr. Sutherland is hardly lying," Erich said. "How would Rosa know that anyway? It's not like Jesus tapped her on the shoulder and told her."

How indeed? Anna thought. Yet sometimes the Lord *did* work in mysterious ways. And, more importantly, she was loathe to dampen her children's trust in God, even as she well knew any supernatural interventions in their lives were hardly forthcoming.

"Jesus does speak to us," she said. "Most times, though, it happens only through our hearts, and it has to do more with how to love and serve Him better than with specific things like sending us someone special. You do understand that, don't you, Rosa?"

"*Ja, Mutti.*" Ever so solemnly, the little girl nodded. "But doesn't Jesus say we're all His children? And that we should welcome everyone like we would welcome Him? Especially a man as kind as Mr. Sutherland? Especially a man He sent to us?"

Sometimes Anna almost wished her daughter wasn't so bright for her age, least of all when Rosa's innocent words forced her to face the truth about her own hypocrisy. Yet what choice had she? It was God, after all, who had allowed life to drive her into such a position. It was God who had permitted the evil in men to destroy her trust in Him and His promises.

But her children didn't need to know what was truly in her heart. Let them keep whatever innocence they still had for as long as they could. Let *them* keep their innocence even if she sometimes wondered whether all her efforts to teach them of a merciful, loving God weren't, in the end, all lies.

"You're right, of course, *Liebling.*" Once more, Anna lowered her gaze to the bandage. "We should try our best to live the way our Lord wants. If nothing else, we should always, always, try."

"You did a very nice job tending Rosa's hand," Anna finally blurted out later that morning as she removed yet another bandage. "I wish to thank you for that, and for coming to her aid."

Ian smiled and shifted his position on the bed to provide her greater access to his side. "At first, she was just as wary of me as ye continue to be. I finally convinced her I meant her no harm. But children are like that. More willing to trust, I mean."

His little jab wasn't lost on Anna. Surprisingly, though, this time it didn't anger her. It was, after all, the truth.

"*Ja,* they're more trusting," she said by way of admission. "But then, they haven't been as hurt or betrayed by life yet, have they? Not like we adults have, at any rate."

"Nay, they haven't." Ian's smile faded. "And I wish they'd never have to be hurt." He turned his head to look at her. "I understand, ye know, lass, why ye try so hard to protect them."

He knows? How could he know? Terror swamped Anna. *Who had told him?*

Her heart thundered in her chest. Her throat went dry. *How could he know about Karl? How?*

She stared at him, looked deep into Ian's eyes. Relief flooded her with such intensity she felt suddenly light-headed. Of course. He was just speaking in general terms about a mother's protective love for her children.

"Then you should also understand why I must be cautious with you," she forced out the words. "Why I must always choose my children's welfare over yours."

"Aye." He turned back to stare ahead. "Or leastwise until ye know me better."

Anna opened her mouth to inform him he'd hardly be here long enough for that ever to happen, when Ian suddenly changed the subject.

"Where were ye born in Germany, lass?"

If nothing else, Ian Sutherland was a most unpredictable man.

Still, the topic of her origins seemed far less inflammatory than continuing to belabor his unwelcome presence. Anna finished unwinding his bandage and laid aside the dressing before answering. "I was born in Mainz, but when I was older and left home, I moved to Rüdesheim where I met my husband. We lived there until we came to America."

"And were ye happy in Germany?"

For an instant Anna's thoughts flew back across the great expanse that was this new land, soaring over the vast ocean separating her from her beloved home. "*Ja.* Though I was very poor, I was happy there," she replied at last, "once I married Karl and came to live with him and his parents. Rüdesheim is on the Rhine River, you know, in a lush, hilly region that's perfect for vineyards. There are ruins of magnificent castles still standing guard up and down the river; and the land abounds with folk tales and mystery and tragedy. I miss the food, too, and shopping in the market overflowing with fruit and vegetables and flowers, and the music, and . . ."

Suddenly aware she was spilling out her innermost longings to a virtual stranger, Anna's voice faded. She grabbed up a clean cloth, dipped it in the water bowl, and began diligently cleaning around Ian's wound. "But it doesn't matter anymore," she then continued. "Karl and Anton decided a better life awaited us in America, and so I'm here. I find my happiness now in my family and in the hope they'll someday have a better life than they ever could in Germany."

"That's why we—my older sister, Claire, and I—also came to America," Ian told her. "Because Claire fell in love with an American, and he wanted to bring her back to his family's ranch in Colorado." He chuckled softly. "And because, at the time, I was a lad constantly in trouble, and my sister hoped to find me a fresh start in a new land."

"And what sort of things did you get into trouble for?" Anna asked, wariness returning to her voice.

"Och, the usual sort of boyish escapades. Fighting. Not attending to my studies. Avoiding school whenever I could." Ian smiled, glanced back at her, then once more looked straight ahead. "I was a restless sort of lad, never knowing what I wanted or should be doing, or where I should be headed."

"That must have distressed your parents." As she talked, Anna applied a light coating of ointment to the wound, which she noted was healing nicely.

"My father had died a long while before, and my mither chose an Englishman over her two children," he replied, his voice taking on an unexpectedly flat tone. "Claire all but raised me."

"Oh." Anna looked up. Ian's jaw had gone tight, his expression grim. There was some sort of sad tale behind that admission, she realized, but to ask more would be to risk an even deeper involvement than she dared to encourage with this man. "I'm sorry to hear about your parents. It must have been very hard for you and Claire."

"Aye, hard enough." As if closing that particular topic as well, he expelled a deep breath. "I missed Scotland verra much, all those years I lived here in Colorado. So much that, when I was twenty-one, I returned home. Bought a little croft house, took up a bit of farming, and raised a few cattle. I lived there for nearly six years, but eventually I again became restless. I sold my land and home, and returned to America."

"And, in all that time, there was never any girl who could win your heart?" Anna thought it strange a man as handsome and well made as Ian Sutherland had never married. Though perhaps it wasn't any of her business—and she knew she definitely shouldn't care—she just couldn't help her womanly curiosity.

"Do ye mean, lass, have I ever taken a wife?"

She could feel her cheeks warm, and was grateful he wasn't looking at her. "*Ja,* I suppose so."

"There were a few lasses, to be sure, who caught my fancy. Still, for one reason or another, things never seemed to work out." As he spoke, Ian's tone lightened once more. "I was in love with Conor MacKay's daughter, Elizabeth, for a long while. Conor's the owner of Culdee Creek Ranch, by the way. But then Elizabeth went off to become a doctor. When she finally returned home, she ended up marrying the town preacher. And then Jean, the Scots lass I was courting for a time in my Highland village, finally tired of waiting for me to pop the question and wed another."

"Sounds to me like there was a reason you put off that proposal." Anna laid a fresh dressing over Ian's wound. "Here, hold this in place while I start winding the bandage."

"Aye, I'm thinking so, too." He half-twisted around to place his hand on his dressing. "My bonny Jean was wise enough to see what I, at the time, couldn't." Ian grinned. "Mayhap, for all my fine hopes and dreams, I'm just not a man meant to settle down."

"*Ja,*" Anna muttered dryly as she began to wind the bandage around Ian's middle. "I must confess to have thought that myself."

He laughed, the sound rich and warm, then caught himself with a sharp breath. "That wasn't the wisest thing to do. Laughing, I mean. Leastwise not with that hole in my side."

Anna tied off the bandage with a small knot. "I'll try not to say anything funny again, then."

"Och, lass, don't hold back for my benefit." Ian turned to fully face her, a roguish light dancing now in his eyes. "On account ye're generally so verra staid and sober, I mean."

Was he laughing at her, or just teasing? Either way, Anna didn't like it. One consideration made her feel like some fussy old woman, and the other . . . well, the other stirred feelings she hadn't felt since before Karl died. Feelings stirred by the realization she was still a woman with a woman's needs, and a very attractive man was, even if in a most subtle way, acknowledging that.

But, truth was, she didn't want to feel those emotions anymore. Karl was dead, and she had vowed to mourn him for the rest of her life. Vowed never to take another man as husband. Not that she had to worry that Ian Sutherland would ever want her as wife. He didn't yet know she was a widow, for one thing, but more importantly, he had just admitted that he wasn't a man meant to settle down.

He was dangerous, nonetheless. Anna knew that now. Before, he had posed a threat just because he *was* a stranger, with a stranger's unknown potential. Now, however, a new peril lifted its ugly head.

Ian Sutherland roused a yearning within her that had nothing to do with common sense or even common decency. He excited her, reawakening long-suppressed needs to be kissed and touched, to be held close to a hard, masculine body, to be loved. Yet, though Anna was honest enough to confront this realization, she also possessed the wisdom not to allow such unbridled—and totally unacceptable—feelings to control her. For so many reasons, she didn't dare.

She pushed back her chair, climbed to her feet, and taking Ian's now mended shirt from the foot of the bed, handed it to him. "Your wound is healing well," she said through stiff lips, steeling herself to the sudden flare of puzzlement in Ian's eyes. "You should be fit enough to leave for town in another few days. Until then, for the sake of rebuilding your strength, I suggest you begin walking about more."

Ian stared up at her. "Lass, did I say aught to offend ye? If so, I beg yer pardon."

The look in his eyes tore at Anna's heart. She knew her abrupt change of mood had wounded him. It couldn't be helped, though.

"You did nothing to offend me," she said, trying to keep her voice cool and noncommittal. "Now, I really must be getting back to my children. You understand that, of course."

"Aye." A sad but knowing look burned in Ian's dark eyes. "I *verra* much understand, lass."

8

That night, sleep didn't come easily for Anna. Visions of Ian Sutherland shirtless, healed of his wound and free of bandages, drifted incessantly through her mind. Visions that taunted her with memories of his well-muscled chest and belly covered with a manly furring of hair. Of his strong arms, his chiseled features, his dark hair curling down the back of his neck, his deep, resonant voice and expressive, compelling eyes.

She tossed and turned in her lonely bed, aching for him, her body on fire with need. Tossed and turned, fighting the temptations that had sprung, unbidden and totally unexpected, into her heart and mind only hours earlier.

"Why now?" Anna whispered, her voice a hoarse disruption of the dark, smothering silence. "Why now, after all this time? Am I ill, or have I finally lost my mind in my grief? And how am I to keep from doing something I must not—dare not—do?"

It had been hard enough getting through those first, agonizing days and weeks after she lost Karl. Just to go on, just to breathe and move her nerveless body. Pretending some semblance of normalcy for the children's sake had been almost beyond her capabilities. And then to go to bed each night, alone, empty, and so very, very frightened with no one—not even herself—to pretend for . . . In those cavernous, terrifying nights she fought the hardest battles for her sanity and survival. Fought them and, she thought, finally won.

But now, now just when Anna imagined she had passed through the worst of it, a new and even more formidable foe had arisen. A foe of the flesh.

Why such a thorn had surfaced now, Anna didn't know. Though she had come to her marriage bed afraid and fighting revulsion, Karl's tender, patient loving soon awakened her to one of the most wondrous aspects of the married life. And, as she had given herself to her husband in all other things, she gave herself just as fully to the most intimate way in which a man and woman could join. But these feelings for Ian Sutherland . . . They were neither holy nor sanctioned by marital bonds.

Was it Satan finally gaining a foothold in a heart that had all but renounced God? It would be so like him, Anna supposed, to try to insinuate himself in such a sordid, most earthly of ways. To use her anger at God, her pride, to undermine her lifelong moral code.

One thing was certain. She dared not risk fighting this new temptation alone. The startling strength of her attraction for Ian Sutherland, an attraction that had overwhelmed her with the force of a tidal wave today, was a warning Anna couldn't ignore.

She slid from her bed to kneel beside it. With a ferocious

intensity, she clasped her hands, then lowered her head to rest upon them.

"*Ach*, forgive me, Lord!" she cried softly. "I should've known if I strayed from Your sheepfold, the Evil One, like a wolf hot on a scent, would come after me. But I was so full of anger and so certain I could make it without You, I began foolishly to rely on my own strength. Take me back, I pray, into the shelter of Your loving arms. And, if it's Your will, send this man and this temptation far from me. I beg this of You, Lord. I beg You, for I don't know how to fight it on my own."

Anna knelt there for a long while, continuing to pray with all the power and fervency she possessed. Yet, no matter how hard she stormed heaven, no answer or peace ever came to ease the despicable feelings she still felt every time she thought of Ian Sutherland.

Finally exhausted and numb from the cold, she climbed stiffly into bed. There she lay, unmoving and no closer to a resolution, until dawn finally peeked over the eastern horizon.

"He needs to leave, Anton," Anna said with adamant insistence late the next morning. "Now. Today. I can't bear his presence another moment!"

From his spot at Anna's side as he helped her wash the breakfast dishes, the old man glanced over his shoulder in the direction of the bedroom Ian occupied. "Keep your voice down, Daughter," he whispered. "Nothing's served by him hearing such uncharitable talk."

Frustration filled Anna. "I don't mean to be uncharitable, but the road to Wolffsburg's surely passable by now. And, more to the point, the man's outstayed his welcome."

"Out-outstayed his welcome!" Her father-in-law all but sputtered his indignant reply. "Ian's only been here three days. And, though you say his wound's healing well, anyone can see he's still weak. What would you have me do? Drag him bodily up onto the buckboard, drive him to town, and then deposit him in a heap in front of the hotel?"

"That was always the plan," Anna muttered stiffly, refusing to be swayed.

"*Ja*, but only when he became strong enough to fend for himself. In case you've forgotten, Ian hasn't a thing to call his own now but the clothes on his back. He hasn't a horse. He hasn't any money. And it'll be at least another week or so before he's fit to do work of any substance. Do you expect him to live on the charity of others in the meanwhile?"

Anna folded her arms across her chest. "Well, isn't that exactly what he's doing here? Living on our charity?"

"*Lieber Himmel!*" Anton threw up his hands in disgust. "What's the matter between you and Ian? I could understand your initial reserve with him, but he's been the perfect gentleman. And have you already forgotten how he came to Rosa's aid yesterday? Yet you persist in treating him . . . in treating him like he's one of those criminals who killed Karl!"

It was Anna's turn to glance now toward Ian's bedroom door. "Keep your voice down, Anton. As far as Ian Sutherland's concerned, Karl's alive and on his way home."

The old man frowned in confusion. "And why ever would you let him believe such a thing? By the time he can be dangerous to you, he'll have surely figured out you lied to him. You'll have accomplished nothing but maybe angering him with your lies."

"*Ach*, Anton!" Anna closed her eyes, so frustrated she could barely sort through the crazed welter of emotions to any remaining shred of logic. "I don't know what to think anymore. All I know is, with each passing day, it gets harder and harder to be near him. I just want him gone!"

"Why, Daughter?" Concern tautening his weathered features, Anna's father-in-law leaned close. "Has Ian not been the honorable man I imagined him to be, or at least not with you?"

Nein, Anna thought. *It's me. I've not been the honorable one. I'm the one who has lusted after Ian, not the other way around.*

She sighed, a long, weary exhalation that embodied all her aggravation and defeat, "Ian has never once made an improper remark or overture. It's me, Anton. It's me."

He cocked his head. "I don't understand."

And I'm too ashamed to tell you the truth. Anna opened her eyes. "It doesn't matter. I just don't want to be near him, that's all. If you insist he stay longer, then you're going to have to care for his wound and bring him his meals from here on out. Until he leaves, I refuse to go near him again."

"Do you know how strangely you're acting, Daughter?" Anton eyed her speculatively. "This is so unlike you that—"

Anna threw up her hands. "I don't care, Anton! I'm sorry if that sounds harsh and unloving, but all I can do some days is just get by. I didn't need this man coming into our lives right now, no matter how brief his time with us might be. I've done the best I can, though, given what I could. I just can't give anymore."

"Did you ever think that, whether you wished it so or not, the good Lord perhaps sent Ian to us? Did you, Anna?"

Did it always have to come back to God? she thought in frustration. And wasn't it bad enough Rosa imagined Ian Sutherland sent by the *Christkindl,* without Anton now trying to find some spiritual reason for his appearance? He was just a man who had happened on unfortunate circumstances, and nothing more!

"I don't think God had any special purpose in Ian's coming here." Anna shuddered. "On the contrary, if anything, Ian's presence here frightens me."

Anton turned, stared down at her. "Are you saying there's something evil about him then?"

She looked away. Why, oh why, wouldn't her father-in-law just let it go? But he seemed determined to get to the bottom of this, no matter if she intended to bite off her tongue first rather then tell him the true reason she needed to avoid Ian.

"Nein," Anna ground out, at the limits of her control. "He's not evil. I never said that. I just don't feel comfortable around him. Will you help me in this, or not?"

Something glimmered suddenly in the old man's eyes, but whatever it boded, Anna didn't want to know. Then he nodded.

"Ja, I'll see to his needs," he replied at last. "Though I don't know how I'm going to explain your odd behavior to him."

Anna expelled an exasperated breath and returned to the dishes. "It's really none of his business anyway, what I do or don't do, is it?" As she talked, she attacked a frying pan with savage vengeance. "He's a guest, not part of the family, after all."

"*Nein*, he's not part of the family. But think on this. He's done nothing to you, Daughter. He doesn't deserve the unkindness you persist in heaping on him. Doesn't deserve it at all."

9

"It seems I'm to be your nurse now."

Ian looked quizzically up at the old man from the length of his bed, where he had just lain back down after several minutes of walking back and forth in his room. "Indeed? I didn't realize I was such a difficult patient, to have already worn out one nurse in the short time I've been here. Did Anna give a reason for her abrupt resignation?"

Anton set the box containing all the necessary medical supplies down on the dresser. "None that made much sense, I'm afraid. I hoped you might be able to share your thoughts on the subject."

Ian frowned. What could he say about Anna that wouldn't offend her father-in-law? Not that Ian thought badly of the woman. On the contrary, he had been battling with himself almost from the first moment he had laid eyes on her. Battling with his strong physical attraction for a happily married woman.

Yet, for all his tumultuous feelings for Anna, he had tried mightily to be honorable in all his dealings with her, never once making improper comments or overtures. He had apparently failed, however, and yesterday's last interaction with her, as she cleansed and redressed his wound, must have been the breaking point.

He scratched his jaw. "Anna's never been overly pleased with my presence here—we both know that. But, bit by bit, I thought she was beginning to tolerate and even relax around me. Yesterday morning, I even managed to get her to talk about her life in Germany. I told her, as well, some things about my past life. Then she suddenly stood up, informed me I'd be fit to leave for town in another few days, and strode from the room." Ian sighed and shook his head. "I still don't know what I said to offend her, save that I teased her about being so staid and sober."

"She wasn't always that way." Anton paused, eyeing Ian intently. "And, though she doesn't want me to say why, I will tell you she has suffered a terrible loss. It's that loss, you know, that colors so strongly how she feels about you."

"I assumed as much. I also gathered it either had to do with Scotsmen or strangers. And I'm willing to wager it also has something to do with her husband." Ian shoved up in bed. "Though she keeps claiming it to be so, her man's not ever coming home, is he?"

The color drained from Anton's face. His lips went taut, and he looked away. "*Nein*. He isn't," he whispered. "My son's dead."

Ian silently cursed his hasty tongue. "I'm sorry. Anna's right, of course. It's none of my business."

"*Nein*." Anton gave a fierce shake of his head. "The truth needed to be told so you'll understand why . . . why we're all the way we are right now. It was a terrible loss. Terrible."

"Aye." There was nothing more to be said. "And the children must have suffered most of all."

"In their own way, *ja*, I think so. But Anna . . ." The old man released a slow, thoughtful breath. "I'll tell you this, Ian Sutherland, but you must never, ever, speak of it with Anna."

Ian wasn't certain he wanted to hear what Anton might next say, but he sensed, nonetheless, that the man needed to share the burden with someone. And, if the truth be told, a part of him hungered to know more about the beautiful, troubled Anna. He wanted to know anything that might help him understand—and reach—her.

He swung his legs around to hang over the side of the bed, gripped the mattress to support himself, then met Anton's gaze. "I won't say aught to her. I give ye my word."

"There were things that happened to her before she came to Rüdesheim and met Karl." Anton walked over, pulled up the rocking chair, and sat. "Things she never spoke about, at least not to me or Freda, my wife, but sometimes . . . sometimes you could see the pain—such pain—in her eyes. Anna was so in love with Karl, though, and I know he made her happy. Even the move to America didn't long threaten their joy, though we knew she was always against it. But when she lost Karl . . ."

For a long moment, the old man looked down. "She finds no peace, no safety, no real pleasure in the world anymore," Anton said, glancing up at last. "She may think she hides her deepest pain from me, but I know she has all but lost her faith—in people, in life, and even in the Lord. And you, my son, are nothing more than another reminder of how precarious her existence has become."

Ian opened his mouth to ask how Anton's son—Anna's husband—had died, then thought better of it. Already, they were both speaking of things Anna didn't want mentioned. He refused to ask for any more details that would cause the old man to further compromise himself. He refused to be the cause of any further pain for Anna either.

"There's no reason I need to remain here another day," he said, his mind made up. "If ye think ye can get the buckboard through the snow, I'm ready to leave for town this verra minute."

"Are you now?" Anton leaned back in the chair and began to rock. "You've suddenly become that strong, have you? Strong enough to put in a hard day's work? Because with not a cent to your name or a horse to take you anywhere, that's exactly what you'd be expected to do in Wolffsburg—if you wanted a roof over your head and some food regularly in your belly, anyway."

"If ye took me to town, I could wire my people who live near Colorado Springs." Ian knew he sounded like a fool even proposing this plan, but all he could think about—care about—was Anna. "Mayhap they could send someone to fetch me, or make arrangements with yer local bank to transfer money."

"Better yet," the old man countered, "while you continue to regain your strength, why don't I go to Wolffsburg and wire your people? If you give me the proper information, there's no reason for you to risk a relapse by leaving too soon."

Ian knew Anton had his best interests at heart. Still, knowing what he knew now, Ian thought it best he hie himself as far and fast from Anna's life as possible. And not just for Anna's sake. If Anna's ongoing struggle to recover from her husband's death wasn't enough, the knowledge that she was now a widow threw everything into a new and even more troubling light.

Anna wasn't married. Anna was free for the taking. And he wanted her. Wanted her badly.

Even now, the memory of her touch as she cared for him yesterday sent a tremor of longing through Ian. And when she had bent close, the fragrance of lavender clinging to her had set his pulse to pounding. He had been overcome with such a powerful urge to move nearer and fill his lungs with the scent of her.

The sudden and unexpected intensity of his desire had made Anna's almost violent rejection of him yesterday all the more painful. Still, Ian had taken it as fitting punishment for his lust for another man's wife. But now the knowledge that she no longer belonged to another fanned Ian's longing for Anna to even greater heights.

What was the matter with him? Had his recent injuries addled him in mind as well as body? Never before had he experienced such an overwhelming need to hold and kiss a woman. It was almost . . . almost as if some hole had opened within him, and Anna was the only one who could fill it. Or, rather, she was the only woman whom he wanted to fill it.

But that made no sense. Ian had all but accepted that he wasn't meant to marry, indeed, most probably didn't even deserve to do so. He was, after all, tainted and couldn't long be depended upon. Sooner or later that old, gnawing emptiness would return. Sooner or later the restlessness, for what he knew not, would arise to torment him until the only respite was found in moving on. To be sure, what woman would ever want a man like him as husband or father to her children?

Not that he had any worry about Anna thinking him husband material. She had made her disdain for his vagabond lifestyle more than evident. And she had never once, he grudgingly admitted, shown any sign of interest in him as a man either.

Still, the intensity of longing she roused in him gave Ian pause. What if . . . what if these feelings didn't arise from within, but were stirred from outside him, motivated by God? He knew the Lord loved him. Knew that He had forgiven him for the horrible crime of his youth. Yet Ian also knew he had yet to fully come to terms with what he had done. He had yet to forgive himself.

Problem was, he was no good to any woman, much less himself, until he did.

"I'm verra grateful for yer offer, Anton," Ian said, forcing himself back to the matter at hand. "However, though I know yer plan is wisest, I cannot in good faith remain here if it upsets Anna so. Until my relations are able to send me money, I'll just have to find some way to get by in Wolffsburg."

"*Lieber Himmel!*" His expression turning dark with exasperation, Anton pushed from the rocking chair. "This has gone on long enough. I'm fetching Anna this very minute and bringing her in here. If it takes us the rest of the day, we're going to work this problem out. *Ja,*" he added with a resolute nod as he turned and headed for the door. "If it takes even until tomorrow, we're going to work this out!"

10

Her fingers numb from the cold, Anna doggedly worked their Jersey cow Lorelei's udders, filling the pail with long squirts of foaming milk. Her mind flew ahead to all the things she must do today, mentally prioritizing them. Though the recent blizzard had most certainly canceled school, she was sure classes would resume again tomorrow, if they hadn't already begun for the children in town. Best that Anton finish digging out the buckboard today so that—

A sharp cry rose from somewhere beyond the vicinity of the barn. Anna halted her milking to hear better. The Jersey cow stomped in irritation, then swished her tail. Several stalls down, the two horses munched contentedly on their hay. Then other voices came—Erich's, Rosa's, then Ian's.

With a sigh, Anna pulled the half-full milk bucket safely out of kicking range and stood. That was all she needed right now—another encounter with Ian Sutherland in front of her children. Still, something was surely amiss for all of them to be outside at the same time. From the sound of their voices, they were upset about something.

The sight that greeted her as she opened the barn door nearly sent her to her knees. There, sprawled a few feet from the house, lay Anton. Ian knelt by his head, Erich and Rosa on either side of him. Anna couldn't tell if her father-in-law was conscious or not.

She set off at a run and slipped on the ice, almost losing her balance. Thankfully, she managed to grab hold of the manure cart sitting near the barn. Righting herself, Anna made her way at a far more sedate pace to where Anton lay.

"It's my right leg," Anton was saying to Ian. "My leg and maybe my back."

Anna motioned the children to move aside, then knelt beside the old man. "What happened?"

"*Ach,* it was the ice," her father-in-law muttered, his features taut with pain. "I wanted to talk with you, and when I couldn't find you in the house, I came outside. I slipped going down the steps, lost my footing, and went flying. I'm not certain, but I may have broken something."

He was dressed only in shirt, pants, and slippers. Anna looked to Erich. "Fetch *Grossvater's* jacket and cap," she said. "And a blanket, too." She next looked to her daughter. "Rosa, go to the woodpile and see if you can find some long, stout sticks to use as splints, will you, *Liebling?*"

As the children scampered off to do their assigned tasks, Anna turned back to Anton. "Where do you hurt?"

He pointed to his right knee. "Here. Maybe I only twisted it. I don't know. And my back . . . It hurts too."

She reached down and began gently to feel his knee. He winced. "Can you move both of your legs?" Anna asked, continuing her way down the limb, then up it, checking for any deformities that might signal a broken bone. "It doesn't appear you've broken anything, and you obviously have feeling in at least one of your legs."

"I haven't broken my back," he said with a wry grin, "if that's what you're wondering. I can feel everything just fine. In fact, a bit *too* fine, if my hurting so badly is any sign."

"Well, I hope it's just bruises and strains. As soon as we get you back inside, I'll head into town and fetch the *Doktor*."

"*Ach,* Daughter, that won't be necessary." Anton tried to lever himself up on one elbow, then grimaced in pain and laid back down.

"*Ja,* it will." Erich arrived at that moment, and Anna proceeded to tug Anton's knit woolen cap onto his head and lay his jacket over him. "In fact, the *Doktor* can have a look at Mr. Sutherland's wound at the same time," she said, finally meeting Ian's gaze. "Perhaps there's more we should be doing to further hasten his healing."

Ian's mouth quirked at one corner. "I'm healing remarkably well, thank ye verra much. Ye're an excellent nurse." He held her glance for an instant more, then wrenched his away to look down at Anton. "In the meanwhile, Anton's not getting any warmer lying out here on the frozen ground. What say ye we splint his knee just as soon as Rosa returns with the sticks, then help him into the house?"

She eyed him uncertainly. "I don't think it's wise for you to risk reopening your wound. Not to mention you're not all that strong yet yourself."

"Anton's a big man. I doubt you and Erich can handle him alone. And besides," Ian added with a grin, "I don't intend to do it all myself. It'll be a group effort, and no mistake."

Albeit reluctantly, Anna had to agree with him. They probably *would* need his help. In Anton's current state, it was unlikely her father-in-law would be able to provide much assistance.

"Well, all right," she said at last. "Just be careful with your side, and don't try to do it all on your own. I don't need two invalids on my hands, you know."

"Aye, lass. I'll be careful. I promise."

Rosa arrived just then with several long sticks. After using the two best ones to splint Anton's right knee, they managed to get him to his feet and back into the house. After settling him in his bed, Anna sent off her son to shovel out the buckboard and Rosa to finish Lorelei's milking.

She then turned to Ian, who had taken a seat at the foot of Anton's bed. "You overtaxed yourself, just as I feared you might. Best you head to your own bed."

The big Scotsman glanced up at her. "I'm fine, just a wee bit out of breath, that's all."

She could feel the tension begin to spiral within her. "Well, *I* don't need you here right now. I've got all I—"

"Aye, ye *do* need me right now," he said, cutting her off. "Ye're just too proud and stubborn to admit it."

Anna's mouth fell open. For a long moment, she just stared at him. How *dare* he speak to her like that, and in her own house no less! She had known from the start he was a contrary—

Anton chuckled. "*Ja,* Ian, I'd say you pretty much—how do you say it?—nailed that one on the head. And, if Anna's too proud to accept your offer of help, I'm not. Though I don't want you overextending yourself, either, mind you. With all the work to be done around here, Anna can't handle more than one sick person at a time."

She glared down at the two men, uncertain if she was being made fun of and assuredly unhappy at being talked about as if she weren't even there. "If you're so bent on accepting Mr. Sutherland's offer of help," she said finally, turning the full force of her ire on her father-in-law, "let him help *you.* I don't want or need his assistance. Erich, Rosa, and I can manage just fine."

"And how much help will the children be, away at school most of the day? Not to mention all the time lost driving them to and from school?" Anton arched a graying brow. "Hmmm, Daughter?"

She hadn't given that eventuality any thought. "Well, maybe they won't be going back to school right away then. Maybe I'll just stop by the schoolhouse while I'm in town fetching the *Doktor* and pick up their books and assignments for the next few weeks until the Christmas recess." The more she thought about it, the more Anna liked the idea. "*Ja,*" she said with a determined nod, "that's exactly what I'll do."

"There are still things the children can't do, and well you know it." Anton's expression went solemn, and he locked gazes with her. "We can use Ian's help, Daughter. And if you won't graciously accept his offer for *your* sake, then accept it for the children's and mine."

Anna wanted to ask what keeping Ian Sutherland around

90

would do for Anton and the children, but she thought she already knew, at least for two out of the three of them. Anton liked Ian and enjoyed the company of another man in the house. And Rosa had gotten it into her head that Ian was sent to them by the *Christkindl*. Erich, on the other hand, remained somewhat wary of Ian and maintained his distance, but Anna suspected that it was more from loyalty to her than from anything else.

Still, Anton was right. Even with his help, it *was* a struggle keeping up with all the chores of a house and cattle ranch, however small it currently was. Without Anton, the workload would be crushing. She couldn't do it by herself.

"Fine," Anna muttered, sighing her defeat. "I thank you for your offer, Mr. Sutherland. You must promise me, though, not to push yourself beyond your limits."

"Ye've my word, lass." Ian smiled. "And ye must promise me one thing in return."

Immediately, Anna's suspicions swelled anew. "*Ja,* and what would that promise be?"

"Naught that I hope will cause ye much discomfort. I'd just like for ye to call me Ian from here on out. If that's not too much to ask, that is?"

Her eyes narrowed. What sort of game was this? And what did he possibly hope to achieve in attempting to set a more familiar tone to their relationship? She didn't trust him and never would. Calling him "Ian" wouldn't make any difference.

"If it pleases you, I can call you Ian," she said. "It won't change anything between us, mind you, but it's a small enough price to pay for your assistance."

"Aye, that's what I'm thinking as well, lass. A small enough price indeed."

Doc Waters put his stethoscope back in his black satchel and snapped it shut. "You're a very lucky man, Anton Hannack," he said as he rolled down his sleeves and buttoned the cuffs. "The ice left by that last big storm is as slippery as the dickens. I've got two ladies and one man in town with broken arms or legs from falling just like you did."

"But there's nothing broken on me, is there, *Doktor?*" Anton asked, leaning forward eagerly.

"No, nothing broken," Doc Waters replied, "but you've really strained your back, twisted your knee, and suffered a severely sprained ankle. It's bed rest for you for the next week, and then maybe only some light walking about for at least another week after that. If all goes well, you might be able to come to town for Christmas Eve church services."

He turned to Anna. "I'm depending on you to make sure Anton follows my orders. Otherwise, there's no telling what that ornery old coot will try."

Two weeks. Anna bit back a groan. Anton was all but incapacitated for the next two weeks. But there was nothing that could be done for it. A body needed time to heal, and an elderly body needed even more time.

"I'll do my very best, *Doktor,*" she said with a tight little smile.

Doc Waters turned to Ian, who stood in the doorway. "I'm glad the Hannacks finally got some sense and hired a hand. This place is just too much for them to manage on their own."

"It *is* a bit of work, to be sure," Ian replied agreeably.

"Well,"—Doc paused to glance at Anton and Anna—"I guess I'll be heading back. Mrs. Murphy and Mrs. Schmidt are both expecting their babies soon. I need to stay close to town as much as I can."

"One moment, *Doktor.*" Anna stepped forward, her gaze skittering off Ian's before meeting Doc Water's once more. "This man has an injury that I thought it best you have a look at."

Doc Waters turned to Ian. "Is that right, Son? Are you hurt?"

"Nay, it's naught." As he spoke, Ian's expression shuttered and became unreadable. "Mrs. Hannack's an excellent nurse, and the wound's nearly healed. Don't trouble yerself over it."

"Suit yourself." The doctor donned his hat and thick woolen coat, then slipped on his gloves. He picked up his bag. "Let me know if you need anything, Anton. If not, I'll assume no news is good news."

"*Ja, Doktor,*" the old man replied. "No news is good news."

Anna followed Doc Waters out to his horse and buggy. The newfangled automobiles had gained much popularity in the bigger cities and towns, and Wilhelm Wolff, town banker and son of Wolffsburg's founder, was a proud owner of the only Model T in these parts. Doc Waters, however, claimed to like the dependability of the old-fashioned horse and buggy. Anna couldn't help but agree with him. Tried and true was good enough for her, too.

"I was serious back there, Anna." Doc paused beside his buggy. "Anton has seriously pulled out his back, and his knee's in bad shape. If he doesn't give everything time to heal, he might cripple himself permanently. I hope that new man of yours plans to stay on for a while. It's the only thing that might keep Anton in bed long enough to mend."

Stay on for a while . . . Anna inwardly winced. That was all she needed—Ian staying on for a while. But what choice had she? She couldn't risk Anton thinking he had to get back to work sooner than he should because she ran off Ian prematurely. Yet to have to endure the Scotsman's presence for another two or three weeks . . .

"I'll do what must be done, *Doktor*," she replied, speaking the words not only to reassure him, but to fortify her own resolve for the hard days—and nights—that lay ahead.

11

That night after the children and Anton were tucked in bed, Anna made herself a cup of tea. Then, taking a seat at the kitchen table, she stared down into her cup for a long while, mulling over the events of the day.

It almost seemed that fate was conspiring to keep Ian Sutherland here for as long as possible. She hadn't wanted to accept his offer of help in the wake of Anton's unexpected injury. If it had just been her, she would have worked herself to the point of exhaustion, and past it, rather than spend even another hour in his presence.

But it wasn't just her. There were Rosa and Erich and even Anton to think about, too. She was responsible for their welfare, their safety, their happiness. Because of that, she couldn't always do just what she wanted. And, because of that, she must struggle a time more with her own demons—and the very real temptation that Ian Sutherland had become.

Anna sighed, picked up her teaspoon, and added some sugar to her tea. "Why, Lord?" she whispered. "Why are You allowing this to happen, when I'm trying my hardest to put this occasion of sin from me? If You think I'm strong enough to endure this . . ." She sighed again. "Just give me the strength then, will You? I don't want to sin. I don't want to hurt You. But I'm just so tormented, so confused by these feelings . . ."

Behind her the door to Ian's bedroom opened, then closed. She heard him hesitate—most likely when he saw her sitting at the table—then head in her direction. Anna closed her eyes, stifling a despairing groan. *Must You test me again so soon, Lord?* she silently asked. *After all that has happened today, I really don't think I'm up for this, You know.*

"Would it be all right if I made myself a cup of tea too," Ian's deep voice rumbled suddenly beside her, "and sat with ye for a time? I can't sleep. Too much on my mind, I suppose."

Anna lifted her reluctant gaze. "*Ja*, if you'd like. I can't promise to be much company, though."

He smiled, and she imagined he was wondering how that was any different than usual. Guilt plucked at her. For all her surliness toward him, Ian had never once—not once—been unkind to her in turn.

"As my people are wont to say, 'dinna fash yerself, lass.'"

Anna frowned. "I don't understand."

"It means 'don't trouble yerself.'"

She stared up at him. Their glances locked and held. Something arced from Ian's dark eyes, spanning the short distance that separated them, to drench her in a most unsettling but not unpleasant warmth. Don't trouble yourself. It seemed, Anna suddenly realized, to embody his attempts, since the first moment he had gained consciousness, to avoid adding to the heavy burdens she already carried. He had always been kind, considerate, and so very appreciative of all she had done for him.

Yet the more he tried not to trouble her, the more he did the very thing he wished not to do. Indeed, the irony of the situation couldn't escape her—it would have been better for the both of them if he had been more the sort of man she first imagined him to be. Instead, Anna was left to deal with a man both enigmatic and engaging. A man who both physically attracted her and repeatedly made it clear he wasn't here to stay, that he didn't stay anywhere, with anyone, for long.

She wrenched her glance from his, pushed back her chair, and rose. "Sit." Anna indicated the chair across the table from hers. "You shouldn't be standing so long. Sit, and I'll get you your cup of tea."

"Nay." Ian's expression darkened in distress. "I didn't invite myself to yer table to have ye wait on me."

"It's no imposition whatsoever. I'm but ensuring you regain your strength as quickly as possible." Her mouth twitched at the corner. "After all, since it now seems you're here for a time more, the sooner you're able to perform Anton's chores, the better it is for me."

Ian chuckled. "Aye, since ye put it that way, I can well see yer point." He pulled out his chair and gingerly lowered himself into it. "It's no more than I want too, lass. To be of some real assistance to ye, I mean. I owe ye and Anton so verra much."

The old impulse to inform him all he owed them was to heal as quickly as possible, then get out of their lives rose to Anna's lips. She didn't, however, have the heart anymore to utter such harsh and unkind words. Even more important, Anna knew she no longer would've meant them.

She didn't dare say, though, what lay so heavily on her heart. She pretended to be too busy getting a cup down from the cupboard and preparing his tea to reply. Finally, though, she couldn't avoid him or the subject of the conversation any longer.

"As much as I was against your presence here, it seems it may well have been a blessing in disguise," Anna said as she returned to the table and set his cup of tea and a spoon down before him. "Not everyone would've been quite so quick to offer to stay and help, especially not after how I've treated you."

Ian didn't look up, seemingly intent on adding several spoonfuls of sugar to his tea. "I knew ye had yer reasons."

"Ja," she replied, blinking back a sudden swell of tears, "I had my reasons. I thought to protect my family."

"No one could fault ye for that, lass."

"No one?" Anna didn't care anymore if her eyes were bright with moisture. "Anton thought I was being uncharitable; I don't even want to consider what God must have been thinking, and you, penniless, far from family and friends, and sick as you were, were caught in the middle of it all. You must have thought you'd fallen from the cook pot straight into the fire."

"I think it's really 'the frying pan into the fire,'" Ian said with a grin. "Still, I won't lie and say yer apparent dislike didn't hurt and confuse me. Nowadays, I can usually get along with most folk. For the life of me, though, I couldn't fathom what I was doing to upset ye so. And that distressed me greatly."

Anna took up her spoon and began to stir her tea. "It was

never you, Ian. It was always me." *And the unholy feelings I felt for you,* she thought, *and feel for you still.*

Indeed, the longer she talked with him now, the stronger her feelings—that aching need within her—grew. Did he, could he, somehow guess?

If ever he realized how confused she was about him, what would he do? Would he pity her or laugh at her? Or, even worse, would he seek to take advantage of the situation and try to seduce her? What were the chances he was like most other men, rather than the rare exception Karl had been?

Even before she had half formed the question, Anna knew the likely answer. Odds were Ian Sutherland, when it came to women, would seize whatever advantage presented itself. And, as harsh a fact as it was for Anna to admit, right now, for reasons she had yet to comprehend, she was so very, very vulnerable.

Even if the need to protect her family from Ian seemed to lessen with each passing day, the same couldn't be said for protecting herself. Indeed, with each passing day, she risked more than just her heart. She risked her very soul.

Five days later, another winter snowstorm moved through the Rockies. The wind howled like a pack of wolves, its blustering force buffeting the little ranch house from time to time. Inside, Ian found it snug and warm. The savory smells of a Sunday beef roast baked in the cast-iron cookstove mingled with the cinnamon-and-apple scent of a pie cooling on the sideboard. The low, happy voices of Erich and Rosa playing a game of jacks before the living-room hearth only added to the cozy sense of family that enveloped him this evening. He hadn't realized how much he had missed it, all the years he had been away from Culdee Creek—the last real home he had known.

From the comfort of one of the two wing chairs, Ian surveyed the living room. It was a cheery mix of German pieces interspersed with the more simple furnishings of a typical Colorado mountain home. An intricately carved cuckoo clock perched on the wall opposite his chair, its long, wooden pendulum swinging to and fro with an energetic purpose. A large, woven tapestry depicting a scene of some village on the Rhine River hung over the fireplace. An assortment of brown pottery jugs and vases filled with dried wildflowers sat beside the fireplace on the left. Family pictures in gilded silver and gold frames graced the fireplace mantle.

Ian rose and walked over for a closer look. On one end of the mantle stood the usual pictures of the children in various poses. A print of Anton and an older woman, his arm protectively encircling her shoulders, also graced the collection.

On the opposite end of the mantle, in a much larger silver frame, was a couple dressed in wedding attire. Even clothed as she was in a simple but elegant wedding dress and long veil, it was an easy thing to make out Anna. The man standing tall and strong beside her must, Ian supposed, be her late husband, Karl. He was handsome, with straight light brown hair and a full beard. His eyes appeared dark, his gaze gentle and full of a quiet strength. Happiness seemed to hover about the couple like some aura.

But of course they'd be happy, Ian thought with a small pang of envy. It was their wedding day, and they had found the love of their lives in each other. The searching was over, the empty hole in their hearts filled. The future spread out before them full of promise, overflowing with potential, their pasts as clean and free of taint as the pure light shining in their eyes. Not like him, whose hands and heart still felt as corrupted now as they did that night so long ago.

The memories weighing heavily on him, Ian turned from the mantle to find Anna standing in the doorway, a quizzical look in her eyes. He quickly stuffed his emotions deep inside him and forced a carefree smile.

"Did ye need me for something, lass?"

In the past days since Anton's fall, Ian had gradually increased the amount of work he could tolerate doing, until he was able to take on almost all of the less strenuous chores. He turned over in his mind the simple pleasures his schedule involved of late. He usually started the day bringing in a load of wood for both the fireplace and cook stove. Then after milking Lorelei, he joined Erich, who helped him hitch the horses to the buckboard, load hay bales, and head out to the closest pastures where the cattle were overwintered. By the time they returned to the house, Anna had an ample, if simple, breakfast ready and waiting.

After breakfast, the pigs were fed the slops from the night before as well as any breakfast leavings. Then Ian helped Erich unhitch the horses and turn them out in the corral. The rest of Ian's morning was spent in simple repairs, while Anna baked the day's breads and Anton worked with the children on their school lessons.

Lunch was an equally hearty meal. Afterward, Ian usually rested for an hour or two, then returned to the barn to again milk the cow while Erich fed the chickens and gathered any eggs. Finally, in the waning light of a mid-December evening, the horses were fed before Ian and Erich headed inside for supper.

"The roast." Anna's soft voice broke into Ian's musings. "If you wouldn't mind, could you get it from the oven, then carve it while I finish mashing the potatoes and making the gravy?" She smiled as if in apology. "I wouldn't ask, but Anton usually does it, and—"

Ian held up a hand. "Say no more. A roast is surely within my limited range of abilities."

The glimmer of a smile touched her lips. "Well, perhaps you should first have a look at the roast. It's a big one."

"Och, lass." He strode over to her. "Fear not. I've yet to meet a roast I couldn't master."

She laughed then, and the sound sent a most pleasant frisson rippling through Ian. Was everything then, he wondered, so utterly flawless and beautiful about her? The light from the kitchen down the short hall threw her face into soft shadows, backlighting her pale hair until her head appeared encircled by a halo. Her blue eyes were luminous, glowing as if with some inner radiance. And her woman's figure, full, ripe, and all sinuous curves, seemed to Ian absolutely flawless.

She seemed, in so many ways, the perfect woman for him. A woman who could, at long last, fill the empty hole in his heart. And, as Ian gazed down at Anna for long, emotion-laden seconds, a terrifying realization insinuated itself into his mind.

Whether he wished it or not, he was falling completely, deeply, and hopelessly in love with her.

12

"So, how are things going between you and Anna?" Anton asked Ian, who had stopped in that evening to pay him an after supper visit. "Is she beginning to see you for the man you really are?"

Ian grinned down at his friend. Anton still had two days left of his initial week of bed rest, and it was becoming increasingly difficult for Anna and Ian to keep him flat on his back. In desperation, they had worked out a schedule among themselves and the children whereby one of them visited Anton at least every two hours during the day, not only to check up on him but to help keep his mind off his bedridden state.

"Things are going pretty well." Ian pulled up a chair and sat. "She seems more relaxed around me and even laughs at my jokes now from time to time. And she doesn't seem in a hurry anymore to get away from me as quickly as possible."

"Hmmm," Anton frowned. "I was hoping for more progress than that." He stared up at Ian intently. "But perhaps you're just as blind in the eye as she is."

It was Ian's turn to frown. "I don't understand. What's there for me to see that I'm not seeing?"

The old man's smile was enigmatic. "And should I be the one telling you? You're smart enough to figure it out on your own, in your own good time. And best you do, too, because I'm thinking my daughter-in-law will fight the truth to her last breath. You've my blessing, though."

His thoughts racing, Ian leaned back in his chair. *He had Anton's blessing* . . . A wild hope flared in his breast. Was the old man intimating he had given his blessing for Ian to court Anna? And was it possible Anton saw something in Anna—a budding affection even—that boded well for such a courtship?

Still, Ian couldn't help think this discussion, at the very least, was premature. He knew Anna well enough now to know any overt attempts at a courtship would quash any chance he might ever have with her. It was also rather disconcerting to realize that the very night he had finally—and most privately—admitted to himself the depths of his feelings for the beauteous Anna, her father-in-law had broached the same subject.

"I didn't know my feelings for Anna were that apparent," Ian admitted at long last.

Anton chuckled. "I saw it coming for a time now. But then, most any man who looks upon my Anna can't help but fall in love with her. You're just the first one I've approved of since Karl."

"But ye don't really know me that well, Anton," Ian said by way of protest. He liked and respected the old man too much to lead him astray as to his true nature. "My feelings for her notwithstanding, I'm not convinced I'm the right sort of man for Anna."

"And why is that?" Amusement glinted in Anton's eyes. "You're a hard worker. You're honest and kind. Rosa adores you, and Erich is fast becoming your friend, too. And you seem a good Christian man. What more could a woman want in a husband?"

What more indeed? Ian thought. Perhaps a man who wasn't tainted by a foul deed in his past? Perhaps a man who didn't keep running from one bright hope to the next, endlessly seeking answers to questions he had yet even to ask? Answers he had yet even to find the courage to face?

He looked away. "Well, if the truth be told, I've always been a restless sort. I don't know if I can ever settle down."

"*Ja*, that *would* be a serious problem in a husband." Anton shrugged. "I suppose then, you must first decide if the treasure is worth the sacrifice. Just don't get so caught up in the thrill of endless pursuit, Ian, that you don't see what you've got right before you. You could end up an empty, unhappy old man with nothing to show for your life."

"It's hardly the thrill that drives me," Ian muttered grimly. "It's more like doubts and fears. That I'm not worthy . . ."

Anton nodded. "*Ja*. I saw that in Anna when Karl first brought her home to meet us. She was like some big-eyed waif, jumping at any unexpected sound or raised voice, trying so hard to please that it soon drove us to distraction. It hurt, it did, to see the depth of her need to be accepted and loved."

"And what did ye do, to help her, I mean?" Ian asked, his heart twisting for the anxious, tormented girl Anna had once been.

"What else? We had to be patient, teach her of the Lord, and then mirror that love to her over and over and over, until she finally began to love herself and give it back in turn." The old man smiled. "Isn't that all any of us can do to help heal the wounds of this world?"

"Aye, I suppose so. Learning to love oneself, to forgive oneself, though, is sometimes the hardest thing of all."

"*Ja,*" Anton said, a sad, knowing light in his eyes, "but how can we ever be whole or give true love or forgiveness to others, if we cannot first love and forgive ourselves? Just as Jesus never gave or forgave in half measures, so must not we. Life must be lived in the fullness of that knowledge. Love must be given unreservedly, without counting the cost, if we're truly to call ourselves the followers of Christ. Love, given unreservedly to ourselves as much as to others."

"I know few men—or women—who love like that." In spite of his effort to contain it, Ian knew an edge of bitterness and frustration had crept into his voice.

"Nor do I," Anton replied, "but my son, Karl, was one of those men. And that's why he was able to bring out the woman who was hiding, broken and terrified, within Anna. The woman who was capable of love, of loyalty, of courage in the face of what was eventually to be such pain and loss."

"And ye think," Ian cried, jealous despair swamping him, "any man, much less the likes of me, could measure up to a man like Karl?"

"We are *all* capable of measuring up to a man like my son," Anton replied softly. "With the help of God's Son and the Holy Spirit, *ja*, we all are. We must just choose to do so. We must just be willing to surrender our pride, our fear, and our willful disobedience, and open ourselves to God's healing love. It's a wondrous gift, to be sure, but one had by all for the asking."

Was that, then, the treasure he had been searching for nearly all his life? Ian closed his eyes and, resting his forearms on his thighs, clasped his hands together and looked down. A treasure, a gift, had by all just for the asking? Anton made it sound so simple, so easy. Yet it wasn't, leastwise not for him. He wasn't, after all, a saintly man like Karl.

"Ye've given me a lot to think about," Ian said, finally opening his eyes and lifting his head. "In the meanwhile, I'd ask ye not say aught to Anna about what we've discussed here tonight. What's between us, after all, is for us to decide and act upon."

"*Ja,* you're right, of course," Anton nodded. "I won't say—"

A knock came at the door. Ian rose to answer it. Erich stood there.

"Aye, lad?" Ian smiled down at the boy.

"*Mutti* asked that you come speak to her for a moment." His glance slid to his grandfather, then back to Ian. "Now, if you please."

Ian grinned. "Tell her I'll be there in a moment." He turned back to Anton. "If ye'll excuse me, it seems Anna has need of me."

The old man waved him his assent. "Go and help her, Son. I can entertain myself."

He almost felt ashamed at his relief in leaving Anton just now, Ian thought as he followed Erich from the room. Their discussion had been intense, touching far too closely to his deepest pain. And the talk of Anna and the man her husband had been only reiterated Ian's feelings of unworthiness, both in loving her and hoping for a life together. Yet how could he make Anton see the truth about him? And what did his stubborn refusal to address his own private pain say about his commitment to Christ?

One way or another, Ian decided as they approached the kitchen, right now wasn't the time to dwell on such matters. Something was afoot and might well need his full attention. It was also, he admitted, a welcome interruption to his troubling thoughts.

At the kitchen table, Anna stood arranging cookies on a tray that already held a pot of tea, a bowl of sugar, four cups, dessert plates, and spoons. She looked up when Ian and Erich entered.

"*Ach,* there you are." She smiled at Ian with such welcome it made his heart give a little leap. "It's time for our Sunday *Adventskranz* ceremony, and since Anton is still abed, we decided we'd carry the wreath and ceremony in to him. We need your help, though, with the wreath."

An evergreen wreath bedecked with four candles sat in the middle of the dining-room table. Ian smiled back at her. "I'd be happy to help in whatever way I can."

"Erich already has a board in the dining room for the wreath." Anna handed Ian a box of matches. "As soon as the two of you put the wreath on the board and light three candles, meet Rosa and me outside Anton's bedroom."

"As ye wish, lass." Ian accepted the matches, then followed Erich once more.

They soon had the wreath positioned on the board. It was quite lovely, bedecked as it was with four sturdy red candles, sprigs of dried wildflowers, and red bows tied on the spruce branches in between the candles. Ian glanced up at Erich.

"Do ye wish to light the candles, lad?"

The boy nodded eagerly. "*Ja,* if you don't mind. *Mutti* usually does it—she's afraid I'll set the wreath on fire again."

"Again?" Ian grinned. "Do ye make a habit of doing that?"

Erich gave a snort of disgust. "Of course not. It happened just once, two years ago, and I'm a lot older now. But you know how mothers can be."

"Aye." He handed Erich the matches. "Have at it, lad."

The smile of gratitude that spread across the boy's face all but erased Ian's earlier turbulent emotions. He watched as Erich lit three candles with the greatest care.

"Why three candles, lad?" he asked. "And why a wreath so soon before Christmas?"

Erich shrugged. "We've always done it. It's a German custom celebrating the coming of the *Christkindl.* And since we don't set up our *Tannenbaum* until Christmas Eve—our Christmas tree," he explained when he seemed to note Ian's puzzled frown, "the wreath is the first real Christmas decoration we put up each year. We call it an *Adventskranz*—Advent wreath—because we set it out on the first Sunday of Advent. That's why there are four candles," he added as he handed the box of matches back to Ian, "one for each Sunday in Advent. And this is the third Sunday of Advent, so we light three. We'll light the fourth next Sunday, as well as again on Christmas Eve."

"It sounds like a wonderful custom," Ian said, watching the flickering candles. "Christmas is such a special, blessed season that we *should* make it a month-long celebration."

"*Ja,* we should." The boy indicated the wreath. "Now, we'd

better hurry and join *Mutti* and Rosa, or they'll wonder where we've gone."

Ian laughed. "Aye, and we'd soon hear about that, wouldn't we? It's never wise to aggravate the womenfolk, is it, lad?"

Erich grinned. "*Nein,* it sure isn't."

Perhaps it was the beauty of the Advent wreath, glowing so prettily as Ian carried it down the hall from the dining room, or the fragrant scent of spruce wafting up to him. Or perhaps it was just the happy light in Erich's eyes, a light of growing trust and friendship, that warmed Ian all the way down to his toes. Whatever it was, he felt comfortable, accepted, and even loved tonight.

It was passing strange that here, high in the Colorado Rockies, with a family so different yet in so many ways the same as the one he had known at Culdee Creek, he had come to this juncture in his life. A life that suddenly seemed so full of promise and potential. A life that just might be the answer to all his dreams.

All he had to do, just as Anton had urged him earlier, was choose it. All he had to do was surrender his pride, his fear, and his willful disobedience, and open himself to God's healing love.

13

Thankfully, the storm was a brief one and deposited only a few inches of fresh snow. The next day the sun was out in full force, and the temperatures rose above freezing. The thaw continued for the next two days, and by Wednesday, almost all the snow lingering from the earlier storm had melted. Anna rose that morning and decided to do the laundry, knowing it would dry by late afternoon if she got it out on the clothesline early enough.

She had Rosa help with the washing and hand her the clean, wet clothes to hang, but once all the laundry was up and flapping in a gentle breeze, she let her daughter join Erich for a bit of play time. The children had pitched in admirably in the week since Anton's injury. Even though their grandfather was now up and about, his chores were confined for a time to simple tasks like folding the laundry, doing the dishes, and setting the table. The children's lessons also took up a good portion of their day, and with their heavy load of chores lately, Erich and Rosa had had little free time to play.

Today, though, was going to be an exception. As she watched

her children head off around the side of the house, a ball clasped beneath Erich's arm, Anna resolved to give them a break from their studies. They could always make up part of the lessons over the next few days, if any catching up was necessary. She was blessed, after all, with very bright and studious children.

Her glance strayed to the laundry swaying on the line. Only a week left until Christmas, and most of the children's clothes were beginning to look pretty threadbare. She needed to get to town and buy them some underwear and socks. She planned, as well, to purchase a few new dresses for Rosa and some shirts and pants for Erich, garments she would put under the tree on Christmas Eve. Anton, she knew, would be happy with a few books and some fresh tobacco for his pipe. And then there was Ian . . .

He had already agreed to stay on until after Christmas, knowing Anton needed time to regain his strength after his injury. Ian had but asked to ride into town someday to send a wire to his family near Colorado Springs informing them he wouldn't be home for Christmas and asking them for a loan of money. He had taken care of that this past week when he accompanied her to town for supplies. Now, however, there was the matter of a Christmas gift for him.

Anna realized she really didn't know Ian well enough to guess what he might like for Christmas. As the days went by, however, what she did know of him she found more and more appealing. The sound of his Scottish burr sent shivers down her spine. It rolled off Ian's tongue like warm honey—or was it more like rough velvet? Either way, Anna never tired of hearing him speak.

And she enjoyed his tales of Scotland, of men in kilts who used to wield claymore and targe in defense of their clans, of the haunting skirl of bagpipes, and of the wild beauty of his Highland home. She shamelessly eavesdropped whenever Ian told evening stories to Rosa and Erich. He came from a proud, fiercely independent people who, quite evidently, placed honor above all else. She saw that now so clearly in everything he did and how he had always behaved toward them.

It would be hard to see him go. She knew that day, though, wasn't far off. Ian had never once intimated he'd like to stay on, or at least not after his obligations to them were fulfilled. That's all it seemed Anna and her family would ever be to him—an obligation his honor wouldn't permit him to shirk.

Anna turned back toward the house. Karl had placed their clothesline on a hill behind the house to catch the full effects of any breezes. From that vantage point, she could just see over the roof of their home to the barn, where Ian worked. Perched high on a ladder, he was hammering a piece of wood siding firmly back into place. Gazing at him, her heart swelled with longing. If only she could convince him to stay on for a while, maybe in time—

From somewhere at the base of the long, steep hill that slid down from one end of the barn, a childish scream arose. Anna paused in her trek back to the house, a chill coursing through her. It was Rosa. It had to be. That was the direction both she and Erich had gone when they dashed off to play.

She gathered her skirts and set out at a run. As she cleared the side of the house, Anna saw Ian—who had apparently also heard the cry—reach the bottom of his ladder and race down

113

the hill. With his long legs, he was far faster than she was, and he soon disappeared from sight.

As she sped along, horrible scenarios played out in Anna's head. A mountain lion lurked in the area. There were surely wolf packs around, too, for she had heard their mournful wails at night. And there was that small, spring-fed pond in a clearing of trees. Drained by her overstimulated imagination and her exertions, Anna reached the crest of the hill with her heart pounding and her breath coming in gasps.

The sight that greeted her, however, all but sucked her remaining breath away. The pond had been solidly iced over less than a week ago, but now a large hole had formed in the center. In that center Rosa flailed, her little hands clutching desperately at the icy ring encircling her. Each time she grasped an edge, however, it would break away. And each time, she slipped beneath the water for a heart-stopping moment before finally, blessedly, fighting her way back to the surface.

From the safety of the pond's edge, Erich stretched a long branch toward his sister. It was too short for her to reach, though, by a good five or six inches. Finally Erich stood up, threw off his coat, and stepped out on the ice.

"*N-nein!*" Anna screamed, quickening her pace until she was all but flying down the hill. It was too dangerous for her son to attempt. She could lose them both. She could lose them both!

"*Nein*, Erich!"

Then Ian was there, tossing aside his own jacket and pulling off his boots. Heedless of surely breaking through at any moment, he ran across the ice. He had to do it, Anna realized, or he would never have a chance of reaching her daughter in time. She watched in horror as Rosa sank below the water once more—and this time she didn't reappear.

Three feet from where Rosa had disappeared, the ice finally collapsed beneath Ian. He went down into the frigid water, then fought his way back to the surface. He took in a huge lungful of air, then dove beneath the water to find her.

Time seemed to stand still as Anna drew up beside her son. He came to her, clutching her tightly, burying his face in her side.

"Ach, Mutti," he cried, "it's all my fault. We were playing ball, and it rolled down the hill and onto the pond. Rosa thought she could get it, and I let her. I let her, *Mutti*!"

Anna pulled him all the closer. Where is Ian? she wondered frantically, her gaze glued to that dark, sinister opening in the ice. How long has it been since he dove down to retrieve Rosa? If he doesn't find her, what will I do?

"Erich." She pushed her sobbing son from her to look straight into his eyes. "Run to the barn and bring back that coil of rope." She shoved him the direction of the hill. "Run. *Schnell! Schnell!*"

Her son stared at her as she threw off her coat and sat down to pull off her boots. *"Nein, Mutti,"* he all but groaned out the words as she climbed back to her feet. "Don't you go out there, too!"

"I have to, Erich." Anna gripped him by the shoulders. "Don't you understand? I have to!"

"A-Anna!"

The voice, little more than a gasping cry, rose from behind her. She wheeled around. Even then, Ian was laying Rosa's limp form on the ice and, with a mighty heave, pushing her toward them.

"Go get the rope!" she screamed at her son. "Now!"

She turned back to Ian. Icicles were beginning to form in his hair. His face was pale, his lips blue.

"What shall I do?"

"G-get down and cr-crawl," he yelled back, his teeth chattering. "I th-think I pushed Rosa far enough—ye sh-should be able to reach her on th-thicker ice."

Anna nodded. Sinking to her hands and knees, she inched toward her daughter. Once she thought she heard the ice groan, then crack, but she made it safely to Rosa. Taking her by one arm, Anna crept back, dragging her daughter along until they reached solid ground. She then pulled Rosa close.

The little girl appeared lifeless. Anna grabbed her coat and wrapped it around her daughter. "*Ach*, Rosa, Rosa," she wept, tears pouring from her eyes. "Don't die. Please, don't die!"

Rosa made a small sound, then began to cough. Choking and sputtering, she expelled what seemed a large amount of water. Anna's heart swelled with gratitude. *Thank You, Lord!*

Anna looked to where Ian still remained treading water. He was strong, but he couldn't last much longer in that freezing water. She put Rosa down, retrieved Ian's jacket nearby, and wrapped her daughter's feet and legs in it.

Then, grabbing hold of the stick Erich had tried unsuccessfully to use, she shimmied out on the ice a few yards and extended the stick to Ian. "Take it!" Anna cried. "Maybe I can pull you out and back to shore."

"N-nay," Ian whispered through stiff lips. "It's too gr-great a risk. G-get off the ice, Anna."

Get back off the ice and do what? Anna thought. Watch him get so cold he finally couldn't swim anymore? Watch him drown? Sacrifice him in order to have her daughter back? It couldn't be. God couldn't ask such a terrible purchase price. He just couldn't!

And then there was a shout, and Erich, followed far behind by Anton, was racing back down the hill, the long coil of rope slung over his shoulder. Anna turned to Ian, a fierce joy flooding her.

"Hang on, Ian," she called to him. "Please, please, hang on!"

14

She looked so peaceful sleeping there, Anna thought, gazing down at her daughter. If not for a few scrapes on Rosa's face and a lingering paleness, Anna could almost imagine the harrowing events of this day had never happened. But they had, and only through the grace of God and Ian's courageous actions had her beloved child been restored to her.

If she had lost Rosa, Anna didn't know what she would've done. It had been hard enough to go on, even for the sake of her children, after Karl's death. She didn't know if she could've survived yet another blow from the same devastating force. Not even for Erich's sake. Not even for God's.

God, though, had always been looking out for her. He had sent them Ian, though he was a gift Anna had at first not only loathed to accept, but had openly spurned. Ian, most likely the only one of them who could've saved Rosa.

Tears filled Anna's eyes and trickled down her cheeks. Ian, kind, generous, and infinitely patient. Ian of the warm, deep laugh and meltingly brown eyes. Ian, the only man, apart from Karl, whom she had ever desired.

She desired him still, but that feeling was intensified now by the admission of her growing affection for him. Ian hadn't even been with them two weeks, yet in many ways—in all the ways that really mattered—she felt she knew all she'd ever need to know about him. As strange and frightening as it was to consider, Anna knew, as well, that she was falling in love with him.

The realization came upon her in those terrifying seconds while she had waited for Ian to resurface with Rosa. She had been, Anna now admitted, nearly as frightened for him as for Rosa, and nearly as panicked about losing him, too. And not just because he was a good man who had risked his life to save Rosa. No, because a light—a special, God-sent, beloved light—would've been forever extinguished.

The tears came again, flowing copiously now as her life flashed before her—the horror, the pain, then Karl, her first bright, beloved light, and such peace, such fulfillment and happiness . . . for far too brief a time. And then the return of the horror, pain, and emptiness. The return of despair, guilt, and unanswered questions until she feared she'd be consumed by it all and never come out on the other side. But she had, only to find another gift awaiting her . . . Ian.

Now it seemed as if Ian, too, would ultimately be taken from her. Not, thank the dear Lord, in death as she had once feared today, but in separation. Would she always, then, be fated to go through life alone and on her own, with no strong shoulder to sometimes lean on, no arms to hold her tight, no kisses and loving to nourish her yearning heart and body?

Anna's weeping progressed to sobs, wracking her until she thought she might break in two. Yet, as hard as she tried to stop it, she couldn't. It was as if . . . as if all the pain and ugliness she had kept locked away from everyone in the deepest recesses of her being had finally broken free.

Then a hand settled on her shoulder. She jumped, twisted about in her chair to look up. Look up into eyes dark with concern, burning with compassion.

Ian.

"I came to bring ye a cup of tea," he said, keeping his voice low. "I thought ye might enjoy it . . ."

Her gaze swung to his other hand, which indeed held a brimming cup of steaming, amber fluid. At yet another display of his caring and concern, Anna's tears, which had momentarily ceased, flowed anew.

"*Ach,* Ian," she sobbed. "You're so g-good to me, and I d-don't deserve it. I d-don't deserve a-anything that's ever been good in my l-life!"

Rosa chose that moment to roll over and mutter something in her sleep. Both Ian and Anna turned to her.

"Come, lass." Ian set the tea down on the nightstand beside the little girl's bed and took Anna by the arm. "This isn't the place to be talking. Let's move out of here."

Anna resisted his gentle but insistent upward tug on her arm. "*N-nein.* I cannot leave Rosa. She might waken and need me."

"She'll be fine for a short while. And if she *were* to waken, she doesn't need to see her mither distraught and weeping her eyes out. At least leave for a short time until ye can collect yerself."

He was right. Her daughter didn't need to see her in such a state. This time, when Ian tugged on her arm, she rose without protest.

In silence, he led her from Rosa's bedroom to the living room. Though it was past ten and everyone else was abed, a fire still burned in the hearth. An oil lamp glowed softly on a small table at one end of the sofa. A book lay open beside the lamp. With a small start, Anna realized Ian had been in here all this time.

She turned to him.

"I couldn't sleep," he said, as if reading the silent question in her eyes. "I was worried about ye."

"About *me?*" She stared up at him, puzzled. "But it was you and Rosa who endured the pond's terrible cold, not me. It was you and Rosa who nearly drowned."

"Aye, but I think it's ye who suffered the most for it, lass." Ian reached up and, with the most tender touch, cupped the side of her face.

More than anything she had ever wanted, Anna wanted to turn her lips to his palm and kiss it. Wanted to press close to him, rest her head on his chest and, just for an instant, pretend that he wanted her, loved her, as much as she wanted and loved him. But it was not to be, and she'd not embarrass Ian by making a fool of herself.

"I'm fine. Just fine." Anna forced a brave smile. "Why wouldn't I be? I thought I had lost the two of you, and you're now both safe and snug tonight."

"Then why did ye say what ye said back there in Rosa's room?" Ian let his hand fall from her face to rest on her shoulder. "That ye didn't deserve me being good to ye? That ye didn't deserve aught that's ever been good in yer life?"

She tried to turn away, but Ian's hand restrained her. A sense of panic clawed at the edge of her awareness. Anna inhaled a resolute breath and turned back to him, covering her rising fear with a false show of bravado.

"I was just upset, that's all. My words meant nothing, absolutely nothing." She glanced down to where his fingers now encircled her arm. "Let me go, Ian. You've no right to lay your hands on me."

A look of pain flashed in his eyes, then was gone. His hand fell back to his side. "Ye're right of course, lass. I've no right. No right at all to care. No right to want to help. And certainly no right to hope . . ."

Hope for what? Anna wondered, as Ian's voice faded and died away. *Hope for what?*

"I'm sorry." She sighed and shook her head. "I didn't mean that the way it sounded. Indeed, if anyone has a right to be treated with decency and respect, it's you. It's just—" her eyes again grew suddenly, traitorously moist, "just that you'll be leaving soon, and I didn't want to burden you with my problems."

"Och, lass, lass," he said. "I'm not gone yet, and I *want* to hear about whatever pains ye. Sometimes in the sharing the burden is lightened, if not altogether eliminated."

"*Ja,*" she whispered, the tears flowing anew, "and sometimes it's better to bear the secret alone, rather than risk losing everything that's good in your life." Angrily, Anna swiped her tears away. "Risk losing your friendship, your respect."

Ian smiled down at her. "And what kind of friend would I be

if I turned from the truth? From something, I'm guessing, that happened in the past?"

A chill washed over her. Anna shivered and clasped herself tightly. "The past makes us what we are today. You can't evade it. It's there, wherever you turn, no matter what you do."

"Come." Ian wrapped an arm about her shoulder, pulling her to him. "Ye're cold. Come close to the fire." He led her to the sofa and gently pushed her down to sit upon it. Then, taking up the knit afghan draped over one corner, he knelt before her and wrapped it around her.

"If ye'd like, I could make ye another cup of tea."

He looked up at her with such a loving expression, Anna wept all the harder. "*N-nein.* I don't need t-tea, I need . . . I just need you to h-hold me." Through her tears, through the hot blood warming her face, she met his startled gaze. She could barely believe she had said that, but she no longer cared. "Pl-please, Ian. Even if only as a friend, I n-need you to h-hold me!"

With a sound that was part acquiescence, part groan, Ian was at Anna's side in an instant, pulling her to him. "Och, lass, sweet, sweet lass, of course I'll hold ye. I'll hold ye for as long as ye wish, for as long as ye need me."

And what if I need you forever, Ian Sutherland? she silently asked. *What if I need you to stay, to love me, to be a father to my children and a husband to me? What would you say then? What would you do?*

Still, though the words rose to her lips, Anna didn't speak them. She couldn't. She didn't dare—just as she had never dared, never found the courage to ever tell Karl the full truth about her past.

But no more! This time, come what may, she'd tell the truth at long last, rip that foul secret from the dark recesses of her heart and lay it open to the light. Ian had said he was her friend. Now was the time to test that claim. Now was the time to take his true measure. If he turned from her in the telling, at least she'd finally know him for the man he really was. A man who wasn't—and never had been—meant for her.

"H-hold me," Anna whispered hoarsely. "Hold me and listen, until you can't b-bear to hold me or listen anymore."

"That day will never come, sweet lass. *Never.*"

"My mother died when I was ten," she began fiercely, almost as if she meant to prove him wrong. "I was left to live with my drunkard stepfather and his shiftless younger brother. I cooked and cleaned and saw to all their needs. It soon wasn't enough, however. My stepfather began to beat me, then eventually took me to his bed, claiming that in my mother's absence I must be a woman to him in every way. It didn't matter that I begged and pleaded, that it wasn't right or natural for a father to treat his daughter in such a way. My pleas seemed only to make him more determined."

She gave a bitter laugh. "Indeed, nothing I said or did moved him. After all, I wasn't his real daughter, he told me. If we had met at some other time, he said he could have married me legally without a second thought."

Her voice caught in her throat. For a moment, Anna couldn't go on. Ian pulled her yet closer, bent his head, and kissed her on the forehead.

"Ye don't have to tell me this. I don't need to hear the rest."

"*J-ja,*" she all but cried out the word, "you do! You said you wanted to know me, to understand me. Well, this is as much a part of me as my life with Karl ever was."

"Then tell me, lass," Ian crooned, his lips soft and warm once more against her forehead. "Tell me and be done with it, once and for all."

Once and for all. An anguished despair flooded Anna. If only it was that easy to purge oneself of such horror, such degradation!

"He forced himself on me over and over again in the next four years. In time, his brother began to bed me as well. They told me I was no good for anything else, that I should be grateful they found any use for me, and after a while, I almost believed them.

"Then one day I couldn't bear it anymore and began to think of killing myself. Thankfully, the minister at the church I attended saved me, when I finally came to the point where I could no longer save myself. Concerned that I had given up attending Sunday services, he visited me one day while my stepfather and uncle were away at work." Anna looked up at Ian. "He was truly a man of God, a man *sent* by God, and I finally confessed it all to him. Knowing it would be hopeless to confront my stepfather and his brother, my minister made plans instead to send me away."

Anna paused, then dragged in an unsteady breath. "One night shortly after my fourteenth birthday, I stole off with my little bundle of clothes and bought a train ticket to Rüdesheim, where the reverend had made arrangements for me to work as a scullery maid in the house of a wealthy doctor. Two years later, I met Karl."

"Did ye ever tell Karl what yer stepfather and his brother had done to ye?"

Anna shook her head. "*Nein*. At first, it wasn't anything I wanted anyone to know about. And later, when I began to fall in love with Karl and saw him for the good, chaste man he was, I feared he'd never love me if he knew the truth. In those days, I thought that I was tainted beyond redemption."

"But when ye came to know the depths of Karl's love for ye, did ye still fear he'd reject ye?"

"By then it didn't matter anymore. It was as if that sordid time had happened to someone else. It was better that way. Better than allowing what had happened to me to sully the pure, beautiful thing we had."

"I think, if ye'd given him the chance, trusted him, Karl could've helped ye heal, lass." Ian crooked a finger beneath her chin and lifted her tear-filled gaze to his. "If his love was truly as deep and wonderful as ye claim it was, he would've *wanted* to."

"*Ja*, knowing him, he would've. But I was a coward and instead chose to bear it alone."

"Until now." He cocked his head, studying her quizzically. "Until this verra night, when ye chose to tell me." A wondering smile touched his lips. "Me, of all people."

"And why not you, Ian? Are you not worthy of my trust? Or has this turned you from me?"

"It'll take far, far more than that to turn me from ye, sweet lass," he said, his eyes smoldering now with some heated emotion. "It'll take ye saying I must leave, that ye don't wish for me to remain here any longer."

126

Her heart began a crazy, irregular rhythm. "And if I never wish for you to leave, what then, Ian Sutherland?"

Joy flared in his eyes, and his head lowered until his lips were but a breath from hers. "Then I'll stay, of course," he replied. "I'll stay because I love ye."

15

After that night, it was as if some heavy weight had lifted from Anna's shoulders, some dark cloud had been blown away by a refreshing, heart- and soul-cleansing wind. She was like a woman reborn.

He knew better, though, than to imagine he was the true source of this transformation. The Lord's loving hand was in this—and had been—from the beginning. Ian was but an instrument in His divine hands.

Still, God was certainly using him in a most pleasant way, Ian thought with a smile three days later as he finished milking Lorelei. A pail of warm, frothy milk in his hand, he trudged back up to the house. All he had to do was show up, so to speak, and the Lord had taken care of the rest. All he'd had to do was be patient, win Anna's trust, and she had finally unburdened herself of her deepest pain.

Not that it hadn't been hard for her. Not that it hadn't required great courage on her part. But who wouldn't understand, wouldn't, in the name of Christ's love, accept her without judging her?

It was the same for him, Ian realized suddenly as he headed up the hill. Wouldn't Anna, in the name of that same love, understand, accept, and not judge him for what he had done as a lad? Yet her "sin," which wasn't a sin on her part at all, had been beyond her control. His, on the other hand, had been deliberate, with full knowledge of the terrible thing he was doing. True, he had felt he hadn't any other choice, that he had to protect his sister, but still . . . still . . .

Sooner or later he must tell Anna about that night. She had exposed her deepest, darkest secret to him. In fairness, he must do so as well. Not that fairness was the only—or even the most important—motive. Nay, he knew he needed a healing as much as Anna. He needed, for some yet inexplicable reason, to receive her forgiveness in order to forgive himself.

It's just so verra hard, Ian thought as he climbed the front porch steps and paused to wipe his muddy feet. Hard to intrude into Anna's happiness just now with his own selfish needs. Needs, he admitted reluctantly, that might change—if not destroy forever—the burgeoning promise of their relationship.

"Just in time, you are," Anna said as she opened the front door for him, apparently having heard his footsteps on the porch. "I'm making *Christstollen* and need some milk." She held out her hand for the pail.

"And I aim to please, ma'am," Ian replied with a cowboy twang as he handed her the pail. "But what's this *Christstollen*? Can't say as how I've ever heard the like of it."

Anna giggled. "*Ach*, but it doesn't sound like you, when you talk that way. I confess I like your Scottish brogue far better."

"Do ye now, lass?" Ian grinned and laid on the accent even more thickly. "Then 'tis the way I'll always be a talkin' from here on out, 'twill. Aught that pleases a bonny lass like ye is reason enough, and no mistake."

"Well, that's all well and good," she said, grinning back. "Just as long as I can understand you, of course." She stepped back and waved him inside. "Now come on in, will you, before you let out all the warm air. After you take off your jacket and those muddy boots, join me in the kitchen, and I'll tell you about *Christstollen.*"

With that, Anna all but skipped away, causing the milk in the pail to slosh dangerously close to the top. Ian watched her go, admiring her slender form, the way she walked with that alluring sway of her hips, and the golden hair piled high on her head. Och, how he loved her! It near to made his heart swell so big he thought it might burst with happiness. He didn't deserve her, but he was no fool, either. He'd not turn from such a gift if it was offered.

He wanted badly to ask her to marry him. Something, though, cautioned him to go slowly for a time more. Though Ian sensed she loved him in turn, Anna had yet to utter the words. When she finally did, the time would be right for a proposal.

In the meanwhile, it was enough to bask in the happy glow generated by two people who very much enjoyed each other's company. It was enough to love Anna, have her know it, and not be rebuffed by her. Indeed, she was far from unreceptive these days. She seemed not only to welcome his overtures of open affection, but to want them, take pleasure in them.

Aye, it was indeed enough . . .

She had measured out the milk she needed and was pouring it into a big green pottery bowl as he entered the kitchen. Ian retrieved a clean milk can from the back porch, poured the rest of the milk into it, then replaced the lid and set the can back out on the porch to chill.

"One good thing about cold weather," he said as he shut the door behind him.

"And what's that?" Anna asked as she cracked two eggs and added them to the bowl.

"Ye can just set the milk outside and don't have to lug it all the way to and from the spring house."

"*Ja*, that's true." She looked up at last. "Come close and I'll tell you about the *Christstollen* as I mix in the rest of the ingredients."

Ian didn't need to be asked twice. He sidled up to stand beside Anna and peered over her shoulder. "Looks like cake batter to me. What's so special about it?"

"It's basically a fruit bread, called Christ or Christmas bread, and I only make it once a year at Christmas. It's filled with almonds, candied lemon and orange peel, and raisins. Then, when the *Stollen's* done baking, I brush it with melted butter and sprinkle it with powdered sugar. It's quite pretty, and the children like it plain or toasted with a little butter."

"I look forward to trying it." Ian rested his chin on her shoulder. "Do ye, mayhap, also make cookies? I confess to a bit of a sweet tooth, especially during the holidays."

Anna nodded, then began to mix the batter, gradually adding in flour until a soft dough formed. "*Ja.* I make *Lebkuchen*—that's gingerbread to you—*Baseler Brunsli,* which is a candy made with chocolate, almonds, and hazelnuts, *Zimsterne,* which are star-shaped, cinnamon-flavored cookies, *Spitzbuben,* which are cookies with jam circles, and *Vanillekipferl,* which are vanilla, crescent-shaped cookies. This is a bit late for me to begin my Christmas baking, but"—she shot him an impish glance—"it's been a most unusual month."

Ian turned his head and gave her a quick kiss on the cheek. "Aye, it has at that, but 'all's well that ends well' as they say. I was just beginning to wonder when ye really began celebrating Christmas around here, considering it's only four days to Christmas Eve and ye don't even have a tree up yet. Ye do put up a Christmas tree, don't ye?"

Ian had already heard about the *Tannenbaum* from Erich, but he found the warmth of the kitchen, and even more so, Anna's warmth toward him, irresistible. He wanted to keep her talking and linger in this most pleasant moment with her as long as possible, so he again asked about the tree.

She chuckled. "*Ja,* considering we Germans were the ones who began the custom of the *Tannenbaum,* or fir tree. It was originally a pagan custom, though Martin Luther frequently receives credit for starting the tradition of the Christmas tree. Unlike a lot of people, though, we don't put up the tree until Christmas Eve. The tree is kept behind closed doors—we'll place it in the dining room—and no one's admitted but me. I'll do all the trimming and prepare the table for the gifts. Then after supper on Christmas Eve, I'll ring a little bell, and everyone will enter the dining room to view the tree. It'll be decorated with tinsel, my precious, handblown glass ornaments, cookies, gilded nuts, and burning candles. Beneath the tree will be our hand-carved nativity figures and stable. We'll sing carols; Anton will read St. Luke's account of the birth of Christ, and then we'll open our presents. Afterward, we'll attend Christmas Eve services in Wolffsburg."

"It sounds like a lovely and verra special night."

Anna began kneading the dough. "I was determined to keep up our special holiday customs. No matter how far one travels from the land of one's birth, I think it's important to remember—and honor—where one came from."

Ian couldn't help but think of the MacKay family harp, given to his sister upon her marriage to Evan MacKay and carried with them from Scotland to Evan's home in Colorado. The haunting songs she would play on that little bogwood harp would inevitably draw him back, each and every time, to the mist-shrouded mountains and glens of the Highlands. And the skirl of the bagpipes . . . well, they stirred his blood whenever he was fortunate enough to hear them.

"Aye," he murmured, a warm sense of heritage and the unbroken continuity of land and family filling him. "In the honoring of one's land and traditions, we honor ourselves and our own special place within them." Ian drew close, slipped an arm around Anna's waist, and nuzzled her neck. "I'm so verra happy and honored ye and yer family have chosen to include me in yer Christmas celebrations. I can't think of anywhere—even home at Culdee Creek—where I'd rather be this Christmas."

She turned her head until she half-faced him, their lips but a breath apart. "*Nein*, it's we who are so very happy and honored to have you with us this Christmas. The children love you so, and Anton is beside himself to have another man to talk to. And I . . ."

When Anna paused and glanced up at him tentatively, Ian's heart slammed against his chest. "Aye, lass," he prompted, "and what of ye? What do ye think about me being here?"

Her lids lowered, then she looked away. "I think you're a wonderful, precious gift. I think"—she lifted her gaze back to his—"I'm the luckiest woman in the world to have a man like you love me. And I think, *nein*, I know, that I love you as well."

Ian's heart swelled with joy. He pulled her around to face him. "Truly, lass? Ye're quite certain, are ye? That ye love me, I mean?"

She arched a brow. "And have you known me to be a woman who didn't know her own mind or who lacked an opinion, Ian Sutherland? Of course I love you! I love you with all my heart."

"Och, lass, lass," he whispered, and taking her into his arms, kissed her long and tenderly.

Anna returned his kiss with an equally ardent one of her own. Time in each other's embrace must have passed far more swiftly than Ian imagined, for there was a sudden, rather loud clearing of a throat from the hallway door. Ian forced himself from his most pleasurable haze and glanced in that direction.

Anton stood there, his head cocked, a benevolent smile on his face. With a jerk Ian released Anna and stepped away. She turned, saw her father-in-law, and gasped.

Her cheeks flaming, she hastily moved back to her bowl of

dough and began kneading as if her life depended on it. Ian looked from Anna to Anton and grinned.

"Aye, Anton?" he asked, fully aware, as Anna apparently wasn't, that the old man was quite pleased with how well their relationship was progressing. "Is there aught I can do for ye?"

"Unfortunately, there is." He gazed at Anna who, head lowered, was still relentlessly working the bread. He rolled his eyes, then looked back to Ian. "The cattle. It's past time we were getting out to feed them. Otherwise"—his mouth curved in a mischievous smile—"I'd leave you two to continue where you left off."

"Anton!" Anna cried, glancing up at last, her face once more becomingly pink.

Her father-in-law shrugged. "And why not, Daughter? You've wasted so much time fighting with Ian, I'd say you have a lot of lost time to make up." He turned on his heel and headed back down the hall. "A whole lot of time," he tossed over his shoulder. "And best you get hard at work on it. Christmas is coming, after all."

16

"Tomorrow is Christmas Eve," Anna said three days later as she finished the breakfast dishes. "I need to pick up a few more things in town today for tomorrow night's special supper. Would you like to ride in with me?"

Ian looked up from his second cup of coffee for the day. He had finished his first one with breakfast before heading outside to complete the rest of the morning chores. Now he was thawing out inside. Yet another storm two days ago had ushered in a foot of fresh snow and below-zero temperatures.

Would I like to ride into town with Anna? He grinned at the thought. *If I had my way, I'd gladly spend every waking moment with her.*

"Aye, I'd like that verra much," he replied instead. "I need to send my sister the letter I finished last night. Not to mention, of course, I'd enjoy the pleasure of yer company."

She smiled. "As would I, yours. Can you be ready in a half hour's time?"

Ian drained the last of his coffee, shoved back his chair, and stood. "I'll get the horses hitched to the buckboard and meet ye in front of the barn in thirty minutes. And besides dressing warmly, best ye bring along some of those lap blankets. In case ye haven't noticed, it's a wee bit nippy outside."

Anna wiped her hands on the dishcloth, removed her apron, and hung it up on a hook beside the door. "As a matter of fact, *ja,* I have noticed. But I've got your company to keep me warm now, and I'm thinking that'll be more than enough."

"Do ye now?" He chuckled, more pleased than he could say. "Well, it's my pleasure, lass, and no mistake." Ian walked over and gave her a kiss on the cheek. "And *that* was also my pleasure," he added before making his way to the front door. He donned his thick jacket, gloves, and Stetson and headed outside.

A half hour later, as the sun was already rising toward its zenith, they set out for town. In Ian's estimation, any time spent in Anna's company these days made for a beautiful day. Still, he had to admit the unspoiled snow complimented the dark green ponderosa pines, gray mountains, and cerulean blue sky to perfection. A man could easily become accustomed to living in this high mountain valley. There was, after all, no end to the unexpected beauty found at every turn of the trail. No end to the unexpected beauty that had overwhelmed his life since he had stumbled upon Anna and her family, and found the love he had so long sought.

Ian glanced at Anna, who was rosy-cheeked from the cold, her eyes bright as she sat next to him on the buckboard seat. "Are ye warm enough, lass? If not, there are those extra blankets in the box behind us."

She laughed. "I'm quite fine. There's hardly any wind, and the sun is actually beginning to feel quite warm. I just pray it doesn't get so warm it melts all the snow again. I was so hoping for a white Christmas, just like the ones we always had in Germany."

He slapped the reins gently over the horses' backs to hasten their lagging pace. The animals increased from their leisurely stroll to a fast walk. "Och, I don't doubt the snow'll stay until at least Christmas. It's not *that* warm."

"And is my big, braw Highlander cold then?" Amusement danced in Anna's eyes. "Aren't you Scotsmen supposed to brave all sorts of inclement weather without giving it a second thought? Or is it that you're just not dressed appropriately and need to put on a kilt?"

"Aye. That's it, lass." Ian smiled and shook his head. "Unfortunately, when I was shot and robbed, the robbers got away with my one and only kilt. Otherwise, I'd be running through the snow in it right now."

"I think I'd very much like to see you in a kilt. You've very handsome legs, you know."

Ian pretended a mock scowl. "And when were ye taking a peek at my legs?"

"Well, when else but when you were ill?" Anna met his gaze squarely. "It wasn't as if we could leave you in your damp clothes. But if speaking of your legs makes you uncomfortable, pretend I never made mention of them. I wouldn't, after all,"—she grinned—"want to embarrass you."

"Ye didn't embarrass me, lass. After all, once ye're my wife, there'll be no secrets or surprises of any kind between us."

At his words Anna's smile faded, and she stared at him with open mouth. Ian's heart missed a beat. *By mountain and sea,* he thought, silently cursing his stupid slip of the tongue. *Whatever possessed me to say that?* It was certainly no way to propose to a woman. On the contrary, it smacked of arrogance, as if he already knew what her answer would be and didn't even need to ask her.

"Lass, . . ." Ian swallowed hard, his throat gone suddenly dry. "I . . . I didn't mean for that to come out quite that way. Please forget—"

"So, are you already regretting that you just asked me to be your wife?" Anna turned in the buckboard seat more fully to face him. "Or did I just imagine that's what you meant?"

"Och, nay, lass!" Ian could feel himself blushing to the tips of his toes. "Ye didn't imagine it. Of course I'd like for ye to be my wife. I only wanted the proposal to come out better when I first asked ye. But instead, what with us laughing and having so much fun teasing each other, it just slipped out. It's what I'd like with all my heart, I mean."

"Would you now?" She tipped her head, studying him. "Well, I think I'd like that, too. To be your wife, I mean."

Ian pulled the horses to a stop, wrapped the reins around the brake arm, and drew her to him. "Och, lass, lass," he groaned, joy swelling his heart. "I'm so glad. So verra glad!"

Anna laid her head on his chest. "I didn't think you were the marrying kind, so I didn't dare let myself hope. But I've dreamed of you asking me. *Ach,* if only you knew how I dreamed . . ."

"I would've asked ye sooner, but I didn't want to rush ye. Ye've been through so much, and I wasn't sure how long ye wished to mourn yer husband. I didn't know how to ask such a thing, either."

"My memories of Karl will always have a special place in my heart." She snuggled close, wrapping her arms about him. "But I know now there's a special place for you in my heart, too. I know the dear Lord has given me a second chance with another good, honest, and honorable man, and I intend to embrace that chance with open arms."

Another good, honest, honorable man . . . Though he knew they weren't meant to, Anna's words stabbed like dagger strokes through his heart. How honest and honorable was he, when he still withheld the tale of his own misdeed?

After all, once ye're my wife, there'll be no secrets or surprises of any kind between us . . .

He inhaled deeply, then took Anna by the arms and pushed her from him. "There's one thing more ye must know about me, about something I once did . . . something that haunts me yet to this day."

She frowned. "I don't understand. What did you do?"

Now that the time he dreaded was upon him, Ian's courage almost fled. *Help me, Lord,* he silently cried. *Ye know I must do this—for myself as much as for her. Just help me tell Anna in a way that won't turn her from me.*

"Our father died while fishing at sea when Claire was five and I was two," he forced himself to begin. "I don't remember much of him. Three years later our mither wed an Englishman, and we were soon all carted off to England. Both Claire and I hated it there. When I was ten, Claire decided to return to Scotland on her own. I convinced her to let me come along.

"Once back in Scotland, we begged our aunt to take us in. Most reluctantly, she did. Neither Claire nor I realized until later, though, the reason for her reluctance." Ian smiled bitterly. "Our uncle, ye see, was a drunkard and physically abusive man. A lot like yer own stepfather and stepuncle, it seems. We lived in squalor, and I eventually ended up stealing just to put food on the table.

"One would've thought it couldn't get much worse, but one night when I was fourteen, after our aunt had died mysteriously, our uncle decided to have his way with my sister. In her defense, I took a stout stick and all but brained the man. Then we dragged him to the sea cliff near the croft house we lived in and tossed him over the edge."

Anna didn't say anything. As the seconds passed, Ian felt his insides twist as taut as a bowstring. Finally he couldn't take the tension a moment longer. "I know this must come as quite a shock to ye, lass, but I want ye to know I've never killed again. It sickened me to do what I did that night, but I had no choice. I couldn't let him harm my sister."

"I know that, Ian." She managed a wan smile. "It's just . . . I just have come to know you as such a gentle man. I suppose, though, even a gentle man would stand up for someone he loves, even if it required force." She sighed. "Indeed, how I wished for someone to defend me when I was in the same situation as your sister. Never would I have wished death on my stepfather and uncle, but I *can* understand why you did what you did. I just have such a horror of violence. You can understand that, can't you?"

"Aye, that I can." He paused, searching for the right words to put her fears to rest. "I'd never hurt ye or yers, though. I give ye my word on that. For a time after that night I'll admit to getting into trouble and causing Claire frustration and heartache, but I was confused and so verra guilt-stricken back then."

"And now, Ian?" Steadily, intently, Anna held his gaze. "Are you at peace with what you did? Have you found it in your heart to forgive yourself?"

The look in her eyes sent a thrill coursing through him. There was no disgust, no fear. There was only concern for him, concern, understanding, and even acceptance. Relief flooded him. *Thank Ye, Lord. Och, thank Ye!*

"I'm beginning to, lass," Ian whispered hoarsely, his throat once more gone tight and dry. "It's been a long, hard road back to that forgiveness, but I think, at long last, I'm finally on my way."

A pensive smile on her face, Anna watched Ian drive away, down Main Street to the post office. This had been a day of crazed emotions. Hers spanned from the heights of happiness, when Ian in his own roundabout way proposed to her, to a troubled sadness when he admitted to killing his uncle. She accepted that he had done the awful deed in defense of his sister. Still, that he had committed such a brutal act at such a young age unsettled her. Did it presage a predisposition toward violence? Or was it but an isolated incident born of unfortunate circumstances?

Everything she knew of Ian assured her he wasn't by nature a cruel or vicious man. And surely, after *her* past experiences, she would've seen some warning signs to the contrary by now. Most likely it was but her instinctive, overly suspicious nature once again rearing its ugly head.

With an exasperated sigh, Anna turned and entered the general store. She had a good bit of shopping to do before Ian returned to pick her up, and time was better spent attending to that than to pointless worrying. Pointless worrying smacked, as well, of disloyalty and ultimately groundless doubts and fears, she realized with a twinge of shame.

As Anna shut the front door, a warm blast of air enveloped her, followed immediately by the scent of wood smoke from the fire burning in the store's potbellied stove. Four of Wolffsburg's most eminent elderly gentlemen, including the town founder, Ferdinand Wolff, were ensconced in the cane-backed chairs clustered about the stove in the store's center. They all nodded to Anna as she passed, then went back to their game of checkers while she made her way to the store's grocery section.

She pulled out her list as Martha Borer finished shelving a box of canned tomatoes. The rotund, pink-cheeked woman straightened her white bib apron and approached, smiling at Anna.

"Haven't seen you in a while," the older woman said. "Been busy getting ready for Christmas, have you?"

"*Ja, among* other things." Anna glanced down at her list. "I'll be needing some cloves, ginger, a bag of salt, five bags of flour, a dozen cans of those tomatoes you just put away, and three bags of sugar."

"Still have some Christmas baking to do?" Martha asked as she began retrieving the items.

"Just what I plan to make for our Christmas Eve and Christmas Day suppers." Anna's glance strayed to the children's clothing displayed nearby. A particularly pretty blouse caught her eye. "Would you mind putting those things in a box for me, Martha?

I still need to get Rosa a few more gifts, and there's a blouse over there . . ."

The other woman laughed. "I understand completely. What with this job, I'm a bit behind on my shopping, too."

Anna smiled and ambled over to the display of children's clothes. She found Rosa's size and picked up a blouse, fingering its smooth, cotton fabric and attractive lace trims. As she did, the conversation around the stove rose behind her and caught her attention.

"Any news about those three bank robbers, Ferdinand? The ones who shot and killed poor Jonas Steckel, I mean?" Sam Neuman asked.

"Talked to Sheriff Mahoney the other day about it," Wolffsburg's founder replied. "Not much of anything new. All they're sure of is the one they shot as he tried to escape is the one who killed Jonas. The posse was never able to pick up his trail again after the bad snowstorm that night."

"Well then," Sam muttered around his pipe stem, "considering the robbery happened December fifth, I'm guessing those robbers are long gone by now. Long gone, I'm sorry to say, with a sackful of the town's money."

Anna's fingers stilled on the blouse. Bank robbers . . . one of them shot . . . December fifth . . . That was the night Anton found Ian wounded and unconscious in the snow!

As if the front door had suddenly opened, a cold chill washed over her. Dread spread its dark, insidious fingers around her heart. It *couldn't* be. She fought against the misgivings, the rising fear. Ian *couldn't* be the third bank robber. It was all just an unfortunate coincidence.

Yet what if it wasn't a coincidence? a tiny voice asked. Ferdinand had said the wounded bank robber was the one who murdered the bank teller. And Ian, just today, admitted to killing his uncle. Was it possible? Instead of a kind, peaceful man, were they harboring a cold-blooded murderer in their midst?

Nausea engulfed Anna, and she suddenly needed to get outside, to fill her lungs with fresh, cold air. She turned and caught Martha's eye. "I—I'll be back in a minute," she all but gasped, then wheeling about, rushed past the men at the stove and out the front door.

For long, sickening seconds she clung to the closest railing, fighting the urge to vomit. Over and over she dragged in gulps of frigid air. Finally the nausea passed, leaving her chilled and sweating. The fear gnawing at her gut, however, remained.

Was it all some horrible lie? Had she never truly seen Ian for the man he was—a dishonest, unprincipled thief? A murderer and liar? Or was she but, once again, allowing her cynical view of life and humanity to color what was, at most, an unfortunate coincidence?

She clenched her eyes shut against the tears welling, unbidden, behind her lids. She wrapped her arms about her, gripping herself tightly. And, through the heart hammering in her chest and the blood rushing in her ears, her chaotic thoughts finally coalesced into one agonizing but rock-hard certainty.

There was no way of really knowing whether Ian was innocent or not. Even if she asked him, she knew she wouldn't trust his answer. But she also knew her doubts would only fester and grow, until they ate away at the very bonds beginning to form between them.

145

In the end, all that mattered was protecting her family. Sooner or later, her heart would mend. It had done so before.

In the end, the only thing left to do was send Ian away. Send him away before it was too late.

Too late, one way or another, for them all.

17

As soon as he caught sight of Anna outside the general store, a box of groceries at her feet, Ian knew something was wrong. He drew up in front of the clapboard building, wrapped the reins around the brake arm, and jumped down. "What's wrong, lass?"

She jerked her troubled gaze to his. "N-nothing. I just . . just want to go home."

Ian was sorely tempted to stand there until he got her to confess to the truth, then thought the better of it. Mayhap Anna wouldn't feel free to talk until they were out of town. He bent down, picked up the box, and deposited it in the back of the buckboard.

When he turned and attempted, however, to place his hands about her waist to help her climb into the buckboard, Anna shrank away from him. The blood in his veins turned to ice.

"Anna . . ."

She swallowed hard, then stepped forward. "I-I'm sorry. Just please help me get up, will you, Ian?"

They were soon driving from town. Ian didn't speak until

they were well into open country. Strange, he thought, that everything appeared as it had on the ride in, yet something had imperceptibly changed between them.

Finally, Ian could stand the silence no longer. He reined in the horses and turned to Anna. "What *is* it, lass? We're far enough now from town that ye should be able to talk. Tell me what's wrong."

"N-nothing, I said!" As if to add emphasis to her words, Anna shook her head vehemently. "I just want to go home, that's all. I need . . . I need time to think."

"What did I do, lass?" Ian refused to let her put him off. Already his rising dread was all but constricting his chest. "Tell me, and be done with it."

She jerked her startled glance to his. "I-I didn't say it had to do with you. I didn't!"

"Ye didn't have to." She had the look of a cornered animal about her. He tried to gentle the tone of his voice. "Yer pulling back when I first tried to help ye into the buckboard said it all."

"Well,"—Anna averted her gaze—"I don't want to talk about it right now. Maybe later, when we get home."

"There's naught that can't be said between us now as well as later. And, if the truth be told, I can't wait until we get home. This change in ye is all but driving me mad." He looked straight ahead, his resolve hardening. "Indeed, we're *not* going anywhere until ye spit it out, so best ye do so straight away."

Beside him, she inhaled a shaky breath and scooted down the buckboard bench away from him. His heart twisted. Had he sounded so forbidding he had frightened her now as well?

"Och, lass." Ian turned toward Anna. "Tell me what's wrong, I beg ye!" He couldn't keep the anguish from his voice. "Now, ye're acting as if ye're afraid of me, and I don't know what I've done to cause it. Tell me so I might make amends!"

"You've done nothing." Anna's face had gone pale, and Ian could tell she was forcing herself to get the words out. "It's just that I've changed my mind about us. I agreed to your offer of marriage in haste, without giving it enough thought."

Relief flooded Ian. "Is that all this is? I can understand if ye need more time, lass. It's all right. Truly, it is."

"*N-nein.*" Once more, Anna shook her head. "You don't understand. I don't need more time. I know now a marriage between us wouldn't work. I . . . I don't *ever* want to marry you. And, now that you're well and have your strength back, I want you to leave my house. I'm sure your family at Culdee Creek will be happy to have you home."

"*What?*" Ian couldn't believe what he was hearing. Anna didn't *ever* want to marry him? And she wanted him to leave, never to return? It made no sense. No sense at all.

He wrapped the reins around the brake arm, then turned back to Anna. "I don't understand. Just a short time ago we were happy in each other's company, laughing, kissing, and ye said ye'd be glad to wed me. And now . . . now ye want me to leave? This makes no sense, lass. It's daft, even."

Hot color flooded her cheeks. "Call it what you will. The truth remains. I don't want to marry you, Ian Sutherland."

The first vestiges of anger warmed the edges of his frustration. "Well, ye at least owe me an explanation for yer mind-boggling change of mind. After all we've been through together, ye owe me that at the verra least."

"I don't owe you anything!" Her hands clenched in her lap, and she began to tremble. "I've the right to change my mind, don't I? That should be enough for you!"

Naught was being accomplished here, Ian realized, but to slowly push Anna to the brink of hysteria. He didn't understand why, but she was acting as if she were now terrified of him. Mayhap, once they got back to the ranch and she had time to calm down, whatever had upset her would lose its grip. Then, Lord willing, he might yet get her to talk to him and explain what was really going on.

"Fine." Ian managed what he hoped was a reassuring, non-threatening smile. "Ye're right. It's a woman's prerogative to change her mind. And we can always talk more of this later."

He turned, untied the reins, then slapped them over the horses' backs. With a snort, the team set off briskly down the road.

Anna didn't say another word until they reached the ranch. Then, not even waiting for Ian to climb down and come around the buckboard to help her, she all but flung herself off and ran up the porch steps into the house. Without a word of greeting, she rushed past Anton, who was kneeling before the living-room hearth adding logs to the fire, and Erich and Rosa doing their lessons in the kitchen. All she saw was her bedroom door.

She threw herself on her bed, coat, gloves, hat, and boots still on, and allowed the long pent-up tears finally to flow. Once the floodgates were opened, however, they didn't again close so easily. Sobs wracked Anna's body. Pain twisted her heart, and that old, all-too-familiar emptiness filled her anew.

Once more she was alone, forced to face life without the love and support of a good, strong man. And she had hoped—oh, how she had hoped—Ian would be that man! Even the consideration of never seeing his smiling face again, never hearing his deep laugh or experiencing the satisfying thrill of that Scottish burr rolling off his tongue, filled her with the deepest sorrow. She longed to feel once again his arms cradling her so protectively against his chest. She had let herself need Ian, crave him even, and now . . . now she must bar him, once more, from her life.

But what else could she do? No matter how fiercely she still longed for him, loved him, her children deserved better than a father who was a killer and thief. No matter how much she was tempted to overlook his terrible failings, she knew her faith wouldn't allow her to condone such sins. Sins he refused to confess, much less offer proper reparation for. To take Ian as husband under such circumstances would dishonor not only Karl's memory, but God as well.

Still, it was hard, oh, *so* hard, to turn from Ian, to let him go, to forcibly drive him away. The look of utter confusion and pain in his eyes when she told him he must leave tore anew at Anna's heart. She didn't mean to hurt him, though hurt him she had. And causing Ian pain, she well knew, wouldn't be the end of it. She still had Anton, Erich, and Rosa left to tell.

Anger filled her. *Never again,* Anna savagely vowed. *Never again will I allow any man to enter my life and heart.* And not just to protect herself, but even more so to protect her family. Protect them not only from the physical, but also from the emotional harm that surely came from loving and having that love found unworthy. From having their fragile hearts ripped asunder as hers had been.

"Wh-why, Lord?" she cried. "Why did you bring this man here, only to take him from us? It makes *no* sense. It's heartless and cruel. Not for me—I deserve nothing—but for Anton, for Erich and Rosa. Why are you punishing them, too? Wh-why?"

She prayed with all her might, storming the gates of heaven for some answer. She wept and wept, beseeching the Lord to help her see, help her understand. After a time, exhausted, Anna fell asleep.

Ian carried in the groceries, placed them on the kitchen counter, and nodded a quick greeting to the wide-eyed children. Then, intent on putting up the horses, he stalked back through the house to the front door. Anton was waiting for him.

"We need to talk."

He could well imagine what Anton wanted to talk about. Ian, however, was in no mood right now to accommodate him. "Later. First allow me to put away the buckboard and the horses. No sense letting the animals suffer just because Anna—" Before he could further snarl out his frustration, Ian bit off his words. "I need some time to sort this all through, Anton. Anna and I had a fight, and I'm angry and confused right now. That's all."

"*Ja,* I gathered that." Anna's father-in-law walked over. "Go ahead, Son. Put up the buckboard and horses. I'll join you outside. Then we can take a walk, okay?"

Though Ian wasn't so sure he'd have his head straightened out in such a short time, he figured nothing Anton would say could make things any worse. On the contrary, the old man might be able to shed some light on Anna's erratic behavior. "Fine. I'll meet ye by the barn when I'm finished."

Fifteen minutes later, Ian and Anton strode off down the road leading from the ranch. They walked for a time in the sunshine and crisp mountain air, both immersed in their own thoughts. At last, though, Anton cleared his throat.

"So, tell me what happened. You and Anna seemed quite content with each other when you left this morning. Then you both came home, and now you're angry and Anna's sobbing her eyes out."

"Truly, Anton, I don't know what happened. On the way to town, I proposed to her, and she accepted. Then I dropped her off at the general store, and when I returned later to pick her up, her mood had totally changed." He shook his head. "She turned cold, like she had been to me when I first came here, and told me she couldn't ever marry me and wanted me to leave."

"Did you ask her why?"

Ian gave a disparaging laugh. "Och, aye. She flatly refused to explain further, except to add that she'd decided a marriage between us wouldn't work. And when I tried to press further, she went deathly pale and acted as if she were terrified of me. It was pointless to press any harder."

"Hmmm." The old man's brow furrowed in thought. "That's most strange. Most strange indeed."

He had hoped Anton would be a bit more help than that. But truly, Anna's behavior *was* unfathomable.

"If ye've opportunity to talk with her and gain any insights,"

Ian began, "will ye share them with me? I love Anna, Anton, and this sudden change in her is most disturbing. Indeed, it scares me. I don't want to lose her, not after how far we've come together."

"I'll talk with her, Son." Anton glanced at him as they walked along. "I'll do my best for you, I will."

"She wants me to leave, and the sooner the better."

"A time apart might not be such a bad idea. It would give Anna some breathing room in which to look at things more clearly. But let me talk with her first."

A time apart . . . Ian didn't like the sound of that. As unstable as their relationship had suddenly become, he feared she might find his absence a little too easy a solution and decide to extend the separation indefinitely. She might go back to her safer and far more comfortable existence and decide she didn't love him anymore.

At the thought, despair flooded Ian. If he should lose Anna now, after finally having found her . . .

It was, in the end though, not for him to decide. All he could do was put it in the Lord's hands. The Lord was, after all, capable of bringing even this miserable situation to a good end. God would do what was best for both of them.

Ian just wasn't sure he wanted what was best, if the best meant losing Anna in the bargain.

18

"Will you be staying for more than one night, Mr."—the hotel desk clerk glanced down at the guest ledger Ian had just signed—"er, Mr. Sutherland?"

Ian pocketed the small stash of bills his sister had recently sent him and met the other man's curious gaze. "I don't know. May I check with ye tomorrow?" He scanned the deserted lobby and large parlor, where a scraggly, forlorn Christmas tree sat. The tree probably looked as bad as he felt, he thought with an equally forlorn twinge before turning back to the clerk. "It doesn't appear, after all, as if ye're bursting at the seams with guests right now."

"No, can't say as we are, it being Christmas Eve and all." The man smiled and handed him his room key. "Tomorrow will be fine, Mr. Sutherland. Just fine."

Ian glanced at his key. Room 10. First floor, probably down at the end of the hall. He headed to his room.

It was noon, and Anton had just dropped him off after begging him not to lose hope, to remain in Wolffsburg at least a few days.

Anton promised, in the meantime, to continue to chip away at Anna. And, more for Anton's sake than for any expectation that the old man would succeed, Ian had agreed.

During the long hours last night, as he lay in bed contemplating every possible reason for Anna's sudden change of heart, the inescapable truth had repeatedly assailed him. With time to think on it, Anna had decided she didn't want a husband, or a father for her children, who was a killer. It was as simple as that.

Ian was surprised Anna hadn't already informed Anton of his tainted past. Mayhap she was saving the news until after Christmas, not wanting to ruin the holidays. Still, he thought grimly, even that made little sense. Seeing the expressions on the children's faces as he and Anton had driven away, Ian doubted there'd be a very joyous Christmas Eve at the Hannack's tonight.

Would Anna, at the very least, be happy now that he was gone? If so, there was some consolation to be had. He had never wished any ill on her. More than anything he had ever wanted, Ian wanted her to be happy.

Mayhap that was why this finally turned out as it had. The Lord had seen what neither of them could, and He knew a marriage between them was doomed. Why that was, Ian didn't know, but he must trust that God did. Must trust and accept.

Mayhap the answers would come tonight, on this the eve of Christ's birth. He'd pray for that with all his might. Pray that the *Christkindl,* whom Erich and Rosa were always talking about, would at least grant him *that* gift, on this most holy of nights.

Anna lit the last candle on the Christmas tree and stepped back to view the effect. Shards of lights glinted from myriad tree boughs, sparkling off the colorful glass balls and bits of silver tinsel. Beneath the tree sat the hand-carved nativity set, with Joseph and Mary kneeling before a yet empty manger. Hannack family tradition was to place the *Christkindl* figurine in the manger after they returned from Christmas Eve church services.

The gifts, wrapped in various shiny red, green, blue, and gold papers, sat on the side table along one wall. In addition to the Advent wreath in the middle of the lace-covered table, cookies, candies, and slices of *Christstollen* decorated a few of Anna's most prized plates. A pottery pitcher of warm, spiced cider and several cups sat beside neatly folded napkins and dessert plates.

As it did every year at Christmas, the room looked festive and beautiful. All that was left was to light the Advent wreath's candles and call in the family. A family, Anna realized with a freshened pang of anguish, which wouldn't be as full or complete as she had earlier imagined it might finally be.

Still, for the sake of her children it was imperative she maintain a happy front. She struck a match and leaned over the table to light the final candles. It wasn't Erich's or Rosa's fault their mother had let her heart overtake her good sense and natural caution. The sooner she made it known Ian Sutherland was but a passing stranger in their life, the better it would be for them.

Anna finished lighting the last candle and straightened. With a resolute lift of her chin, she turned and headed for the door. To her surprise, the children weren't standing there, impatiently jostling for the best spot to peer into the dining room when the door opened. Fact was, they were nowhere to be seen.

Frowning, Anna made her way to the living room where Anton was ensconced reading his Bible. "Have you seen Erich or Rosa?"

Her father-in-law looked up. "I think they're in their rooms. Do you need them for something?"

"*Ja*, the *Tannenbaum's* lit, the treats are ready, and the gifts are laid out. I thought we could see the tree, eat some sweets and all, a bit earlier this time. To cheer the children up . . ."

"It'll take more than Christmas customs to cheer them up this year." Anton closed his Bible, rose, and tucked the Book beneath his arm. "But if that's what you want, Daughter, I'll fetch the children and bring them to the dining room."

She knew he wasn't any happier with her right now than the children were. In one of his rare moments of anger, he had even raised his voice a time or two when she had remained steadfast in her determination to send Ian away, all with no explanation other than the one she had already given Ian. But Anna had also known if she revealed her suspicions about Ian, her father-in-law would've laughed them to scorn and immediately gone to Ian and told him everything.

In time, though, they would all forgive and forget. They would understand she had done what she did to protect them. Meanwhile, Anna would bear the burden in silence and love.

It seemed Anton took an overly long time fetching the children, but Anna at last heard them coming down the hall. She swung open the dining-room door and waited in eager anticipation. Erich came first, shooting her a sullen look before averting his gaze. Rosa followed, her eyes red, her face blotchy, as if she were recently crying. And then there was Anton, shrugging apologetically.

Anna inhaled a steadying breath and squared her shoulders. This might take a bit more effort than she had first imagined. She smiled, stepped into the dining room, and gestured to the brightly gleaming fir tree.

"Isn't it beautiful, Children? I think it's the finest tree we've ever had, don't you?"

Erich paid the tree a cursory glance, then walked over, picked up a cookie, and bit into it. *"Ja, Mutti,"* he replied unenthusiastically. "It's very beautiful."

"It's because Ian helped us find it," Rosa piped up just then. "*That's* why it's the finest tree we've ever had." Her lower lip trembled. "But now he's never going to see it all decorated and pretty."

"Grossvater," Anna said, knowing her daughter well enough to guess the wailing would soon begin if they didn't quickly distract her, "why don't you read us St. Luke's Nativity passage? Then we can sing carols before we give out the gifts and eat some sweets."

The look her father-in-law sent her was a dubious one, as if he were convinced anything she tried tonight was doomed to failure. Still, he pulled up a chair, sat, and opened his Bible. "And it came to pass in those days," he began, "that there went out a decree from Caesar Augustus that all the world should be taxed . . ."

Erich and Rosa drew close, leaning over his shoulders to read along with him. Anna's heart swelled with love. They were all so dear to her. They were all she had.

She knew they were hurting and confused. She couldn't blame them. She just hadn't the heart to tell them the truth about Ian. Maybe in time, but not just now. Let them at least get through this Christmas with some peace and joy for the season. In the end, after all, it wasn't about them, but about the *Christkindl,* the holy child born on this holiest of nights.

Tears filled Anna's eyes as Anton finally reached the verse where the angels spoke to the shepherds, crying out "Glory to God in the highest, and on earth peace, good will toward men."

Angels that night had been God's heralds, announcing to the shepherds that a Savior had been born. Angels came in other guises, too—as guardians, helpers . . . and even as strangers sent to test a person's devotion to God.

"And would you turn away a brother in need, Daughter? Would you turn away an angel unaware?"

What *was* that verse of St. Paul's Anton alluded to on the night of Ian's arrival? Ah, yes: "Be not forgetful to entertain strangers: for thereby some have entertained angels unawares." As far as her father-in-law was concerned, Ian was one of those angels. But Anton didn't know what Ian had done as a lad, or that he most likely was one of those bank robbers, either. Anton could only trust in God's mercy. Anton could only trust in the potential goodness of a stranger.

Anton had shamed her into taking in Ian that night he had come wounded and helpless to them. He had shamed her into agreeing out of a spirit of Christian charity, out of love for God and her fellow man. And for a time, in coming to know Ian, Anna thought she had rediscovered that charity and love. Her tightly guarded heart opened once more and, like a flower, she had bloomed, found renewed joy. She had fallen in love.

Then a few overheard words slammed shut the doors of her heart. She had known the truth without even asking another question or offering Ian a chance to explain. She had just *known* she was right, and that he had, all along, been unworthy.

As unworthy as Anna had secretly always known *she* remained. She had never deserved a good man. It was why Karl had ultimately been taken from her, why Ian surely could never be a good man. And that dirty little secret—that she herself was the unworthy one—had remained firmly imbedded in her heart, woven throughout her love and admiration for both men.

With a sudden, breath-grabbing insight, Anna realized her own sense of unworthiness had made her secretly blame herself for Karl's death—a tragedy that hadn't, in any way, been her fault. And because she had also felt unworthy of Ian, it had been an easy—oh, *such* an easy!—leap to accuse him at the very first opportunity. Indeed, if she hadn't heard that story in the general store, Anna knew she would've soon found another reason to condemn Ian—not because *he* deserved it, but because *she* didn't deserve him.

In the candlelit room with the air redolent of pine, Anton finished the Bible passage and began softly to sing the beloved carol "*Stille Nacht*," first in German, then in its English version, "Silent Night." As she watched a tear course down her daughter's cheek, Anna's throat tightened in anguished self-reproach. In her misguided attempt to protect her children from life's pain, she had inadvertently shielded them, as well, from life's opportunities for happiness and love. From the experience, as Karl was wont to put it, of a God-permeated life full of unexpected beauty. In her misguided efforts to protect herself and hide her secret unworthiness, she had clung overlong to her unwillingness to risk her heart, to trust, and to forgive. In the doing, she had also condemned a man who had never, ever, been anything but honest, kind, and loving to them.

She had repaid his gentle generosity with suspicion, refusing even to give him a chance to defend himself. The only truth that had mattered was the truth *she* chose to believe. Even if Ian *had* done the terrible things she feared, it didn't lessen God's command to love him as her brother. A love that owed him the truth, even as she deserved the same from him.

"I was wrong," she whispered. "Wrong to have sent Ian away without giving him a chance to defend himself."

Anton glanced up, his eyes widening in surprise. "What did you say, Daughter?" Beside him, Erich and Rosa looked at her and went very still.

"I heard some talk at the general store yesterday. Talk about three men who robbed Wolffsburg's bank on St. Nicholas Eve. One of them was shot escaping. I thought that man must be Ian."

"Then you would've been wrong, Daughter." Her father-in-law rose, laid his Bible on the chair, and walked over to her. A sad, knowing light gleamed in his eyes. "After I left Ian today, I stopped by the feed store to pick up some corn for the cattle. While I was there, Sheriff Mahoney came in. They found the three robbers holed up in old Max Elder's cabin. The one who was shot was just finally on the mend, hence the reason they stayed so long in these parts. Seems they were three brothers down on their luck and looking for an easy way out of their troubles."

Why had she, deep down, already known this? That Ian had always been innocent? Anna smiled. She had known it just as soon as she had faced her own sense of unworthiness and cast it aside, once and for all.

"*Ja*, I was wrong," she said softly. "But Ian's gone, and now I'll never have the chance—"

"God is far more merciful than you deserve," her father-in-law cut in brusquely. "Though you've made a terrible mistake, a *stupid* mistake, there still might be a chance to redeem yourself. I convinced Ian to remain in town tonight, in the very hope you'd somehow find your way through the darkness that seemed, once more, to have overtaken your soul."

A wild joy flooded Anna. "Ian's still in Wolffsburg? In spite of my cruel treatment, he was willing to wait on me, give me another chance?"

"*Ja*, I think so. I *hope* so." Anton cocked his head, doubt suddenly darkening his eyes. "He wasn't in the best of moods when I left him, though. I hope he didn't decide to up and head out toward his home in Culdee Creek."

"Well, shouldn't we be getting dressed and heading out to Wolffsburg a bit early ourselves then for Christmas services?" Erich offered of a sudden as he strode over to his mother. "Just in case Mr. Sutherland is still in town, I mean. He might like to come to church with us."

Anna looked down at her son. At the firm decisiveness shining in his eyes and ringing out in his voice, her heart swelled with pride. *Ach*, but he was so much like his father, he was.

"*Ja*, you're right, Son," she said, her heart near to bursting with joy. "We need to ready ourselves to go to town."

19

It was a crisp, clear night, the sky an ebony swath pierced by sparkling bits of light. A full moon illuminated the snow-covered road, bathing the shaggy pines, boulders, and rock-strewn mountains in silver radiance. Silence lay on the land, a reverent, expectant, holy silence. As it must have all those many centuries ago on the night of Christ's birth, Anna realized, overcome with awe.

There was an expectation of another kind this night as well. One of whether she would find Ian still in Wolffsburg. Of whether he would find it in his heart to forgive her for her cruel and unfair treatment. And of whether he could still love her.

The sound of voices lifted in song caught her ear as they arrived at the outskirts of town. As they drew near the center of Wolffsburg, Anna could see a huge fir tree decorated with colorful paper garlands, gilded nuts, pine cones, and strings of popped corn. It stood in the middle of the town square. Torches blazed around the tree and, standing before the torches, warmly dressed carolers sang.

She smiled. Every year, it seemed, Wolffsburg's Christmas celebrations grew a little more festive. She half expected one day to see a German *Christkindlmarkt* here, laden with all sorts of handcrafted Christmas gifts and traditional baked items to buy. A Christmastime market that would entice folk from towns as far as the plains and beyond, even.

Her Christmas musings were drawn up short, however, as Anton reined in the horses before the hotel. Anna's heart began a wild clamoring beneath her breast. *Dear Lord, help me,* she prayed. *I'm not ready. I don't know what to say. What if Ian rejects my plea for forgiveness? What if he no longer loves me?*

Then there was no time for further questions. Erich jumped from the buckboard, helped his sister down, then turned to his mother. "Come along, *Mutti,*" he said, lifting his arms to her. "We really haven't much time before Christmas services, you know. And we've still to find Mr. Sutherland and invite him along."

She turned to Anton. "Do you want to come in with us? If so, we can wait for you in the lobby."

He shook his head. "*Nein.* Best you and the children fetch Ian. Erich's right. We've got maybe fifteen minutes before the bells ring for services. I'll wait here for your return."

Anna had hoped her father-in-law would choose to accompany them inside. Somehow his strong, solid presence would've provided the support and encouragement she needed so badly right now. But then, *she* had been the one who had caused all this trouble. It was only fair, Anna supposed, that she be the one to stand alone to make amends.

Not that she'd really be alone, she thought with a grin as she followed her children into the hotel. Their happy, excited presence would surely buffer any potential unpleasantness that might arise between Ian and her. Indeed, no one, not even that dour-faced clerk at the front desk, could long be unmoved by her children.

"I'm sorry," the man was saying to Erich as Anna drew up behind her son, "but I'm not at liberty to divulge the names or the room numbers of our guests."

"Well, then, go and fetch him, please. His name's Ian Sutherland." Erich shot a quick, surreptitious look at the hotel ledger. "He's sure to be expecting us by now."

Anna bit the inside of her cheek to keep from chiding her son for lying. And perhaps Ian *was* expecting them, or leastwise hoping they'd soon come. According to Anton, Ian had agreed, after all, to remain in Wolffsburg a few days in the hope she'd have a change of heart.

"Is that true, ma'am? Is Mr. Sutherland expecting you and your children?"

Suddenly all eyes, including the clerk's, were riveted on Anna. She swallowed hard, then nodded. "That's what my father-in-law led us to believe, didn't he, children?"

Both Rosa and Erich nodded solemnly.

"Well . . ." The clerk hesitated, then grinned. "I suppose it's all right then. Mr. Sutherland's in Room 10, down at the end of that hall." He pointed to a long corridor to his left. "Merry Christmas."

Relief flooded Anna. "And Merry Christmas to you, too, sir."

With a whoop of joy, Erich dashed off down the hall, his sister hot on his trail. Anna rolled her eyes, smiled apologetically at the desk clerk, then hurried after them. By the time she caught up with her children, they had already knocked several times.

Rosa's eyes were huge as she glanced up at her mother. "He won't answer, *Mutti*." Her lower lip began to wobble. "Maybe he's still mad at us."

"More likely he has already given up and left town," Erich muttered darkly. "We're too late, and it's all your—"

His dire pronouncement directed at his mother was abruptly cut short as the door before them opened. Ian stood there, his shirt unbuttoned, towel in hand, wiping the last vestiges of shaving cream from his cheeks.

For a stunned, speechless moment, they all stared. Then, with a ragged clearing of her throat, Anna took each of her children by an arm and pulled them behind her. "H-hello, Ian," she croaked. "I . . . I came . . . I came to apologize for my unkind and most stupid behavior of the past two days. I don't know what got into me, but—"

"*Mutti* was a *Dummkopf.*" Rosa chose that moment to pipe up helpfully. "I heard *Grossvater* call her a *Dummkopf,* I did, and I think he was right. Don't you, Erich?" she asked, leaning around Anna to find her brother. "Think *Grossvater* was right?"

Anna could feel her cheeks flame. This wasn't at all how she had envisioned her meeting with Ian would begin. "*Ach,* Rosa," she said between gritted teeth, "this is one time you'd do best to be seen and not heard. What I have to say to Ian is between him and me, not you or Erich."

Her daughter hung her head. "I'm sorry, *Mutti.*"

"Well, if it's any consolation, Rosa," Ian offered just then, "I kind of think yer mither was acting a bit of the *Dummkopf,* too." He met Anna's startled gaze and grinned. "Still, it took a lot of courage for her to come here tonight, and ye must always remember that and be proud of her.

"Isn't that right, Anna?" he then asked, turning back to her with an arch of his brow.

At that moment, she didn't know whether to throttle her daughter or Ian, or just take her children by the hands and march back down the hall the way they had come. But then common sense—and a good dash of humility—filled her. She *had* been a *Dummkopf* to treat this wonderful and yet most maddening man the way she had.

"I don't know how courageous I am," she finally replied, "but I do know when I've made a terrible mistake. I heard some things that I thought involved you, and in my fear and confusion, I chose to run from you and the happiness you offered. I guess I just thought it easier to return to the old ways of looking at people and life than to fight my way back to the trust and love you showed me."

His eyes burned with compassion and understanding. Burned with such a light, Anna realized, that she imagined them to look like Christ's eyes would in gazing at her. With a light of acceptance, forgiveness, and love—oh, such love!

"I'm so s-sorry, Ian," she whispered, her voice breaking. "Please, I beg of you. Please forgive me."

"Och, lass, lass," he crooned, reaching out to stroke her cheek with an inexpressibly tender touch. "I never blamed ye. I thought it was me. That I had turned ye away when I'd told ye about . . . about that night."

Beside her, Erich heaved a big sigh. "So, have you two made

up yet? And are you going to come back and help us at the ranch again? Because it's almost time for Christmas services, and I'm getting tired of standing here listening to all this sweet talk and stuff."

Ian chuckled and tousled the boy's hair. "Just give yerself another four or five years, lad, and ye'll never be tired of sweet talk and stuff again." Then he lifted his glance back to Anna's. "And, whether I'm to come back and help at the ranch is entirely up to yer mither. She knows, though, that ye children need more than a ranch hand, Son. Ye need a father. But that's up to yer mither too . . ."

Excitement rippled through Anna. Was he really asking her what she hoped he was? There was only one way to find out.

"I love you, Ian." She met his gaze squarely. "I'd like very much to be your wife, if you're still of a mind to have me. And if you're not, I understand. Truly, I—"

"*Wheesht,* lass." He laid a finger to her lips. "Of course I still want to marry ye. I've never stopped loving ye. Never."

With a soft cry, Anna flung herself into Ian's arms. He held her tightly to him, his lips touching the top of her head. And as he did, bells began to toll, filling the night with their joyously exuberant sound.

"Come on," Erich cried. "It's time. Time to welcome the *Christkindl!*"

Without awaiting Ian or his mother, Erich grabbed Rosa's hand and began tugging her down the hall. With one final hug, Ian released Anna. "Give me a moment to button my shirt and put on my coat, and I'll be ready."

As she stood there in the doorway and watched him, a deep

peace engulfed her. She was so blessed, far, far more than she'd ever deserve no matter how hard she strove in life. But to bless abundantly was and had always been God's way.

On this holiest of nights, Anna thought, He had come down in the form of a small, helpless baby, intent on growing up and living among us in order to bring all to salvation. And not because any deserved it. No, only because He loved us. Loved us with such a deep, abiding, wondrous love. In turn, all she or anyone had to do was accept that love, then return it to anyone they might ever meet in this life. Give . . . in the same measure, with the same generosity, as they had been given.

"Shall we be going, lass?" Ian, dressed and with a radiant smile on his face, joined her. "We don't want to keep the children waiting, do we?"

"*Especially* not on Christmas Eve. And then, after services, we all need to go home, we do. We've still got gifts to open, and carols to sing, and treats to eat."

"I'm verra much looking forward to that, I am," Ian said as he closed his door, then took her by the arm and started down the hall. "German Christmas customs are all so verra lovely. Of course," he added with a grin, "when it comes to New Year's celebrating, we Scots have a few amusing tricks of our own up our sleeves."

"I can't wait to hear about them." Anna laughed out loud. "*Ach,* but it's going to be such fun being married to you, Ian Sutherland!"

"Aye, of that ye can be sure, lass," he said, laying on a thick brogue. "Verra, verra sure."

Their laughter, as they reached the end of the hall and entered the lobby, even made the clerk, scowling over his ledger, smile. And then Anna and Ian were outside. After helping her onto the buckboard seat beside Anton, Ian climbed up to sit next to her.

The older man winked at Ian. "I'm glad you decided to stay on for a while."

Behind them, Erich laughed and clapped his hands. "This is the best Christmas ever!"

"*Ja,* it sure is," his sister replied, sticking the end of her braid in her mouth. "And, just as we hoped, the *Christkindl* has given us the best gift of all."

Her brother's nose crinkled in puzzlement. "And what gift is that?"

"*Ach,* Erich, don't be such a *Dummkopf!* On this most blessed of nights," Rosa explained with exaggerated patience, "the *Christkindl* has answered our prayers. Just as we asked Him to, He has sent us a Christmas angel—in the gift of a new father."

Dear Readers,

Hope you enjoyed Ian's and Anna's story. I'm the kind of person who always likes—indeed, feels more comfortable with—closure, and I knew from the moment I finished *Child of Promise*, the fourth book in my Brides of Culdee Creek series, that sooner or later I'd eventually have to find Ian his own true love. Ah, that wonderful sense of closure! I couldn't think of a happier ending—or should I say, a happier beginning?—for Ian.

Since I wanted to do another novella centered around Christmas, and ever mindful of my German heritage on my mother's side, I thought a German heroine and her family would make for some very special characters in *The Christkindl's Gift*. Many of the German names that appear in this book, by the way, are those of my German ancestors. Anna Hannack was my maternal grandmother's maiden name. Anton was my maternal grandfather's name. Karl, Erich, and Rosa were also names of some of my ancestors, as was the passing mention of the name Thimm. Rüdesheim, Anna and her family's German home, was one of the many lovely towns I visited on the Rhine River when I was stationed in Germany with my husband. And several of the Christmas customs practiced and recipes mentioned in *The Christkindl's Gift* were ones I grew up with, too.

As far as future books go, I know I've been promising some Scottish stories about the MacKay family ancestors. They will come in time but, in the meanwhile, I'm working on an entirely new series set in the Scottish Highlands during the time of Mary, Queen of Scots. The first book, *Child of the Mist*, will be available in February 2005, so you don't have long to wait. What can I say? I'm a sucker for a man in a kilt.

Excerpts of *Child of the Mist* and all my other previously published books are available on my website at http://www.kathleenmorgan.com. And I'm always happy to hear from readers. To be included on a mailing list (either postal or email) with updates on future books, write to Kathleen Morgan, P.O. Box 62365, Colorado Springs, CO 80962 (a self-addressed stamped envelope is always appreciated) or email me at kathleenmorgan@juno.com. Overseas readers need, instead of stamps, to include international reply coupons purchased at their local post office to cover the cost of postage.

Blessings,

Kathleen Morgan

Sauerbraten

I thought you might enjoy trying some of the recipes mentioned in *The Christkindl's Gift*. The first one, *Sauerbraten*, is but one version of this delicious rump roast dish. It's great with mashed potatoes, cooked mashed carrots and turnips, and red cabbage and apples (see below). It's one of my favorite meals. Serves 6.

4 pounds rump roast	3 bay leaves
2 tablespoons shortening	3 whole cloves
2 onions	2 tablespoons catsup
½ cup vinegar	¼ teaspoon pepper
1 cup water	2 teaspoons salt
2 tablespoons lemon juice	Gingersnaps, 10–15 crumbled to taste

Sprinkle roast with a little salt, pepper, and flour on all sides, then brown in shortening and onions. Add remaining ingredients except gingersnaps. Cook covered on low for 2 ½ to 3 hours. About ½ hour before serving, remove bay leaves and cloves, then add crumbled gingersnaps to make gravy. Remove roast from pot, slice, and pour gravy into gravy boat to serve over meat, mashed potatoes, and mashed carrots and turnips if so desired.

Red Cabbage and Apples

Here's another one I love, red cabbage and apples, and it goes great with *Sauerbraten*. Serves 6–8.

4 cups shredded red cabbage	1 tablespoon sugar
⅓ cup white wine (optional)	1 teaspoon salt
⅓ cup cider vinegar	½ teaspoon caraway seed (optional)
1 medium tart apple, peeled and diced or sliced	

Mix ingredients well in pot. Cook on medium-low heat for about 45 minutes or until cabbage is tender, stirring occasionally. Let stand covered for 10 minutes before serving.

Christstollen

I had to give you a recipe for *Christstollen*, after making such a big deal of Anna making it in the book. For all the candied fruits, etc., in it, it really is a bread, though, and probably better enjoyed that way, plain or toasted with a bit of butter. *Stollen* is sold in many stores at Christmas. Makes 3 loaves.

1½ cups raisins
1 cup chopped citron
1 cup chopped candied orange peel
½ cup rum
2 envelopes dry powdered yeast
½ cup lukewarm water
1 tablespoon sugar (optional)
2 cups milk
1 cup sugar
2 teaspoons salt
1⅓ cups butter

grated rind of 1 lemon
2 tablespoons rum
2 cups flour
4 eggs, lightly beaten
5–7 cups flour
1 teaspoon almond extract
1½ cups chopped blanched almonds
melted butter
granulated sugar
confectioner's sugar

Combine raisins, citron, and candied orange peel and soak in rum 1 hour. Drain and reserve rum. Dissolve yeast in warm water according to instructions on package, using a little sugar to speed the process if you like. Scald milk with sugar, salt, and butter. When the butter has melted, stir in lemon peel, rum, and almond extract. Cool mixture to lukewarm. Add yeast and 2 cups flour. Mix well and set in warm draft-free corner about 15–30 minutes or until dough blisters. Stir in lightly beaten eggs and gradually mix in 5–7 cups flour until dough is soft and light but not sticky. It should be smooth enough to be handled.

Dry soaked fruit and dredge lightly with flour. Turn dough onto a floured board and knead, gradually working in fruit and blanched almonds. Knead dough until it blisters and is smooth and elastic. Gather in a ball and place in a lightly floured bowl. Brush with melted butter. Cover loosely with a thin kitchen towel and set in warm, draft-free corner about 1 hour or until it has doubled in bulk. Punch dough down and cut into 3 equal pieces. Set aside to rest 10 minutes. Roll or flatten each third of dough into an oval ¾ inch thick. Brush top of each with melted butter and sprinkle with a little sugar. Fold each lengthwise, not quite in half, so that edges are within ½ to 1 inch of meeting. Pinch closed. Place loaves on a buttered baking sheet or jelly roll pan. Brush with melted butter and place in warm, draft-free corner again so they can rise until doubled in bulk, about 1 hour. Preheat oven to 425 degrees. Bake loaves 10 minutes, then turn heat down to 350 degrees. Bake about 45 minutes, or until loaves are crisp golden brown. Brush with butter and sprinkle generously with confectioner's sugar while warm. Cool and sprinkle with more sugar before serving.

Zimsterne

Cinnamon stars or *Zimsterne* are a popular German Christmas cookie. Makes about 40 cookies.

3 egg whites

½ pound fine, quick-dissolving granulated sugar

3 teaspoons powdered cinnamon

1¾ to 2 cups grated unblanched almonds

½ teaspoon almond extract

finely ground nuts or fine granulated sugar for pastry board

Preheat oven to 300 degrees. Beat egg whites and, as they begin to get foamy, gradually beat in sugar. Continue beating until whites stand in very stiff peaks. They should retain the mark of a knife blade. Set aside ½ cup of whites to coat the cookies. Sprinkle whites with cinnamon and almonds and add almond extract. Stir together gently but thoroughly. Mixture should be heavy and fairly solid. Add more almonds if it is too sticky to be rolled out. Sprinkle pastry board with nuts or sugar and roll out dough to about ¼ inch thickness. Cut into star shapes with a cookie cutter. Place on greased baking sheet and spread a little of the beaten egg white on each cookie. Bake about 30 minutes. Cookies should be golden brown and slightly chewy.